D0407074

THE FAN

THE FAN

by

BOB RANDALL

Random House 🏠 New York

Copyright © 1977 by Bob Randall

All rights reserved under International and Pan-American Copyright
Conventions. Published in the United States by Random House, Inc.,
New York, and simultaneously in Canada by Random House of Canada
Limited, Toronto.

Manufactured in the United States of America

Acknowledgments

The author wishes to express his gratitude to
FREYA MANSTON, BRET ADAMS and JANE RICHMOND
for their help and enthusiasm.

To JULIA and EDWARD

THE FAN

THE FAN

Characters

SALLY ROSS	Ex-movie star, at present star of Broadway musicals
BELLE GOLDMAN	Sally's secretary for the last six years
JAKE BURMAN	Sally's ex-husband of seven years, a producer at Continental Studios
STAN JOHNSTON	A New York City detective
HEIDI BURMAN	Jake's present wife, twenty-four years his junior
DAVID	A young man who becomes Sally's lover
BRET LAIRD	Sally's agent
JO AND SYLVAN COLTON	Friends of Sally's
LILYAN PETERS	Ex-movie star, friend of Sally
PHIL	An old friend of the fan
CHARLES STERN	Real estate agent for the co-op apartment house in which Sally lives

3

EDITH PATERSONN	Sally's next-door neighbor
CAPLAN	New York City police captain
BESS ASHER	Belle Goldman's sister

and

DOUGLAS BREEN	The Fan

4

BRET LAIRD Ltd.
25 East 57 Street

Jan. 25, '76

Dear Sal,

The script arrived from Dino De Laurentiis. It's interesting, but frankly I don't see it as a star vehicle. I'm sending it on to you anyway. Will you please return my calls? Much as I love chatting with Belle and hearing all about her voluminous family, I still need to know how you feel about the last paragraph on the *Tatters* contract, which should have been signed weeks ago. Also, *Who's Who in the Theatre* arrived, noticeably missing your birth year. You been talking to the Gabors lately?

Bret

SELTON, MARKS & LANDAU REALTORS
1231 Avenue of the Americas

January 26, 1976

Dear Miss Ross:

We've had several complaints now from other shareholders in The Bradford about the noise coming from your apartment in the early hours of the morning. We do understand the need for a star such as yourself to unwind at unconventional hours, but for the sake of your neighbors, could you try to do it more quietly?

Thank you.

Charles Stern

January 26th, 1976

Dear Miss Ross:

I don't know if you remember me, but I'm the young man who last wrote you several weeks ago, to congratulate you on your new show, *So I Bit Him*, soon to go into rehearsals. I know it will be another hit, as only you can give Broadway. I was wondering whether you had any new photographs taken recently. If so, I would love one for my collection.

Your greatest fan,

Douglas Breen
780 West 71st Street
New York City

7

JO COLTON

Dear Sal,

Just a bread and butter note to tell you that Sylvan and I had a wonderful time the other night, at least as much as we can remember of it. You really will be the death of us.

Jo

P.S. Are you or are you not coming out to the island for your birthday? And are you bringing someone? And if you are, what can we expect? Gay or straight, male or female, or that person nobody was sure about?

P.P.S. Sylvan says he was sure. It was a transsexual who changed his mind. Sometimes I think I'm too old for this world.

Dear Jo,

Sal asked me to let you know she can't make it. Too much to do in town. And just between you and me, I think this is one birthday she'd just as soon skip. It's the big five-o, near as I can figure out.

But ask her again, will you? She could use a few days off. I'll get her to bring someone really kicky—female, straight, a hell of a lot of laughs. Me. I could also use a few days off. Tell Sylvan I can still beat the pants off him at backgammon and he still owes me twelve bucks from the last time.

                                                    Belle

P.S. Jake wrote Sal that he'd love to hear from you two. He's at Continental now. Did you know he got married again a few weeks ago? Sal took it pretty well, at least what she let on, but if you ask me, she's still got a case on him herself. That and the big five-o coming at the same time aren't doing her ego any good. But you know Sal, she'll bounce back like always.

1412 Fairview Terrace

Dear Miss Ross,

My daughter is seventeen years old and recently announced to her father and me that she no longer intends to go to college, but wants to try for a career in the theater instead. We were heartbroken and pleaded with her to be sensible. Surely the theater is no place for an immature girl of seventeen. If, after she completes her education, she still has the desire, then she will have our blessings. Don't you agree that her education comes first? I thought that perhaps if you were to write and tell her so, she might listen to you. My husband and I are terribly upset. We love her very much and worry about her future. Her name is Jeanne. I know it's a lot to ask, but a letter from you might mean a great deal.

Thanking you in advance,
Mrs. Mildred Broaten

Sally Ross

Tuesday the 6th.

Dear Jeanne,

Your mother wrote me about her concern over your plans to go into the theater before completing your education. Jeanne, no one is more enamored of the theater than I am. I know how worthwhile and fulfilling it can be, but I also know that the theater makes many demands, and one of these demands is preparation. There are few places a fledgling actress can learn her craft these days, and a college theater is one of the best. I think it would be a great mistake to let this chance slip by you. A career lasts a lifetime, Jeanne. Surely it's worth preparing for properly.

Yours,
Sally Ross

CONTINENTAL STUDIOS

Feb. 9, 1976

Dear Sal:

Yesterday, while I was hiding out from all this damn southern California sunshine, I dug out our old marriage certificate. I thought I'd have it bronzed and send it to you for your birthday. Then I saw your birth date on it.

Welcome to the fifties, baby.

Do yourself a favor, huh? I know how you react to birthdays. Don't do a number on this one. There's a chance I may fly in at the end of the month for a couple of days. If I do, I'll bring Heidi with me. I want you to meet her. You'll like her, Sal. She's a sweet kid.

Now I've got to get back out into that sunshine. Jesus, don't they ever shut it off?

Love,

Jake

12

Sally Ross

Dear Jake,

You son-of-a-bitch. I will not be anywhere remotely near fifty. I will be forty-six. And I ought to know. After all, I've been forty-six several times now and I recognize it. So I don't give a rat's ass what the marriage certificate says. Incidentally, my darling, what are you doing holding on to that old thing? We had it revoked years ago, you know.

I still love you, as always.

Dolores Gray told me she had lunch with you and your new missus the other day in old L.A. Dolores said she's quite a knockout, despite the teeny hint of cross-eyedness. (Is that a word?) Excuse the bitchiness but ex-wives are allowed, especially when ex-husbands marry girls young enough to be my sister, you rat. I love you even more now that you belong to someone else. (Heidi? Her name is really Heidi? Does she have braids? How is she on milking goats?)

Listen, if you bronze the certificate will you at least have the decency to ink out my age first? For old times' sake?

I love you a lot, you groom you.

Your Gal Sal

13

P.S. Belle says congratulations on the wedding, better luck this time, take Vitamin E and hold your stomach in. She also says it's indecent of us to go on writing to each other now. Belle is likewise a rat.

February 17th, 1976

Dear Miss Ross:

I couldn't possibly let your birthday go by without wishing you an Oscar-Tony-Emmy winning day! You are the greatest star in the firmament and your birthday should be a national holiday with schools let out and cheering in the streets!

Not to sound self-interested, but I haven't received that photograph yet. And I've cleared the most perfect spot for it in my studio apartment. If you could send it, it would really make my day. Again, congratulations, congratulations, congratulations!

Your greatest fan,

Douglas Breen
780 West 71st Street
New York City

Sal:

Hors d'oeuvres are in the oven. Just turn it on to 250 for about twenty minutes. You do know how to turn the oven on, don't you? It never occurred to me to ask.

That big thing in tin foil on the counter is a five-foot Italian sandwich. I picked out most of the anchovies but if I missed a few, don't yell at me, I've been busy and a little protein couldn't kill you.

Sorry I can't be there to help, but I've got est, and Werner Erhard waits for no woman. We're low on rum so don't get fancy with the drinks. Also, don't forget, the car comes to get you at nine-thirty for Philly, so kick the gang out early. And hold it down, will you? You got neighbors. I won't be in til around eleven, so don't forget to set the alarm like you always do.

Listen, at midnight go into the bathroom, lock the door, turn on all the faucets full blast and wish yourself a secret happy birthday from me. Then look in the stall shower. A little present from your secretary. Don't be embarrassed, it only cost me an arm and a leg. Happy forty-sixth. (Now, there's a real present!)

Belle

February 19th, 1976

Dear Miss Ross:

This morning I woke up with a slight fever and so didn't go into the record shop where I work. Instead, I spent the day in bed watching TV. I know it's a bore, but what else can one do with a cold? And there, before my delighted eyes, on *The Mike Douglas Show*, was the most glamorous, vivacious star of them all. You! I was, needless to say, thrilled beyond words. But tell me, what with the rigors of preparing for rehearsals, those endless conferences and your necessary social obligations, do you really think you should go all the way to Philadelphia to plug the show? Wouldn't it be wiser to use those blessed off hours for relaxation and rest? Or is the producer of *So I Bit Him* a slave driver, as is my boss? You looked, I'm sorry to say, tired and that upset me. Please take care of yourself. There is no replacement for you.

Your greatest fan,

Douglas Breen
780 West 71st Street
New York City

P.S. I still await the photograph.

Dear Penthouse C,

Look, I'm sorry for the words we had in the elevator yesterday, but you really got my goat. I've been Sally Ross's secretary for six years and believe me, she's a hell of a person and not at all what you said. So let's bury the hatchet, okay? Next time Sally lets off steam with a few friends, come on over and join the party instead of ratting to the cops. You'll like her. And I make the best stinger this side of Trader Vic's.

So, friends?

Belle Goldman

EDITH PATERSONN
941 FIFTH AVENUE

Feb. 21.

Dear Miss Goldman,

Thank you so much for your very kind invitation to join in Miss Ross's bacchanals, but my husband and I prefer revels of a quieter nature. Especially at three in the morning.

Mrs. Patersonn (Penthouse C)

Dear Mrs. Patersonn,

Fuck yourself.

Mrs. Belle Goldman

Sally Ross

Belle,

There's paté in the refrigerator for lunch. Just pretend it's liverwurst and enjoy. Had to leave for an interview at the crack of dawn. Please, please try to remember to get my goddamn stationery from Tiffany's. I'll be reduced to writing people on toilet paper soon. (Also, there's a surprise in the package for you.)

The pictures arrived. Please autograph them and get them out. And before I forget, what possessed you to tell the gargoyle next door to fuck herself? Honestly, Belle, and at your age?

Sal

Sal:

What do you mean at my age? My age is your age minus two, in case you forgot.

I sent off the pictures, I told Bret you'd call him sometime before dawn, I got the laundry, I got your gown (they did a crappy job on the hem), I ate the royal bologna and I'm off to the Bronx now to get the hell off my feet. See you in the morning. By the way, your stationery is on the kitchen counter. Thanks a lot for mine. I'll be the only woman in the A & P with a grocery list written on Tiffany paper. (Hold on to your money, will you? Stop buying me expensive things I don't need.) Incidentally, I told her to fuck herself because I'm too much of a lady to tell her what I really meant.

Belle.

Listen, don't go in the dining room. I polyurethaned the floor. You're welcome.

February 25th, 1976

Dear Miss Ross,

Or might I call you Sally?

The picture arrived and it's gorgeous! You always look fantastic in white! I went directly to a frame store as soon as it arrived and selected a simple Lucite frame to house it. It looks fabulous on my dresser. Just the touch this place needed!

Again, Sally, thank you, thank you, thank you!

Your greatest fan,
Douglas Breen
780 West 71st Street
New York City

23

Sally Ross

Monday the 26th.

Dear Jake,

This letter comes to you from the crankiest old lady the world has seen since Mrs. Macbeth. I started off this black Monday by snapping at Belle like a fish wife over nothing at all. Well, not precisely nothing at all. She started a war with her highness nextdoor and I'm caught square in the middle. Know anyone who wants a penthouse cheap? Oh, Jake darling, what a day! I wouldn't let up on Belle until I made her cry. Why does she put up with me? Why doesn't she get a job in a nut house, where people are easier to get along with? What a pair we are. Two old ladies who make snappy retorts instead of getting laid.

Then, having spat my venom at Belle, I went over to the Algonquin to meet Gideon Riggs, the choreographer for *So I Bit Him*. Just a little get-acquainted lunch. Nothing could possibly go wrong, right? Wrong. After an hour or so of toying with a shrimp, I realized my appetite as well as my disposition was ruined. Or rather two shrimps. Mr. Riggs, it turns out, is all of one foot tall, give or take an inch. I'm sure they found him under a toadstool. And lucky me, he was desperate to tell me about a number he'd already worked out in his miniature head for the show. He said the routine came to him in a dream, and by the look on his face, I'd say the dream was more than slightly moist. I am to do an entire number comprised of—are you sitting? —cartwheels and splits. You heard correctly. Me. Cartwheels and splits. I explained to the munchkin that I don't do cartwheels and only stocks split these days. He explained to me that there was nothing to it. Inside of two days he'd have me looking like an Olympic gymnast. (Think of it, Jake, I'll finally be asked to do grapefruit juice commercials!) I explained to him that there are these things called bones, and I've got some, and I'd like to keep them in precisely the shape they're in at the moment.

Well, a pall fell over the Algonquin that eventually oozed out into the street and all the way to Bergdorf's. Good lord, are we going to have fun in rehearsals, the miniature schnauzer and I. If I hadn't already signed the contract, I'd ship out in a road company of *Arsenic and Old Lace* (the Josephine Hull role, of course). Oh, Jake, I'm so old. I look like what's left in Grant's Tomb. Sometimes I look in the mirror and see Judy's face staring out at me, the way she was in London. It won't happen to me, will it? No, Belle wouldn't let it happen. If I so much as hint that I wouldn't take offense at an offer of a second drink she opens that mouth of hers. Bless that mouth. And I had to make her cry like a complete witch. What a sight Belle and I will make one of these days. Strolling through the park, heavily veiled, humming "Send in the Clowns" and hitting strangers with our canes. Oh darling, don't you just love it when I feel sorry for myself? Well, why the hell not. Gretel, or whatever her name is, has you and all I've got is eight per cent of the gross. Can you believe they tried to get me for six? Is there no sense of fair play left in the world?!

Cartwheels and splits. I'll make Ripley yet. Well, it's time to apologize to Belle again. It's the third time she's been at the refrigerator in the last five minutes.

I love you but it sure doesn't solve my problems.

Your Gal Sal

Dear Doug,

Surprised to hear from me? I know I haven't written in a while, but old friends are allowed to be lazy, aren't they? The reason for this letter is first of all to say hi and second to tell you that Ginnie and I will be in New York on the third for two days. We'll be staying with her parents at 885 West End Avenue. I don't remember their number and Ginnie is at school now but you can look it up. Their last name is Pryor, in case you've forgotten.

Listen, old buddy, I don't like to be pushy, but Ginnie would get an enormous kick out of meeting Sally Ross, and so would your old buddy here. Since you're her best friend and a big wheel at the record company she records for—got the message?

I promise not to embarrass you in front of her. I won't even mention those great old days in Camp Kawana-loonah. So, what do you say? Is it a date?

Phil

March 1st, 1976

Dear Phil,

    Bad timing. Much as Sally would love to meet you and I'd love to spend some time recalling those grand old days of yore, no can do. I've simply got to get Sally away for a few days to rest up before rehearsals of *So I Bit Him* start. That's her new blockbuster, you know. I've read the script and it's sensational! But rehearsals are a killer. It's gruel, gruel, gruel all the way. We plan to leave tomorrow night so, unfortunately, we'll be gone! Luck is no lady to-night!

    But Sally insisted I pass along her latest photograph, suitably inscribed, of course.

    Hope you have a good time in the Big Apple.

Your friend,

Douglas Breen
780 West 71st Street
New York City

Dear Sally,

Something really awful happened!

I was late for work the other morning and had to
dash. Well, to make an endless story short, I forgot to
unplug my toaster, which is the old-fashioned kind, and I
had a small fire. No, there's nothing to worry about. Luckily only a few odds and ends were ruined, but alas and
alack, your photograph was among them! So here I sit
among the charred ruins with a broken heart.

I know how expensive those "glossies" are, but I'd
give my eye teeth for a replacement. Is there any chance?
I'd gladly reimburse you for the cost.

Your greatest fan,

Douglas Breen
780 West 71st Street
New York City

CONTINENTAL STUDIOS

Mar. 2, 1976

Dear Sal:

Knock it off. You're as gorgeous as you ever were and you know it, so stop looking for compliments. Besides, what do you want to be, a tortoise? They don't age, but they also don't look like you do. No joke, baby. Like the man says, you're not getting older. Just better.

As for me, I'm in the doghouse at the moment. We had Bob and Lola Redford to dinner last night and Heidi was a little overawed by them. Maybe that's why she didn't say a word for a solid hour. Not one syllable. When they left I mentioned it to her but it must have come out a recrimination because she started to sulk and say it was my job to ease her into the conversation. I tried to tell her they're just people but the more I talked the sulkier she got, and, I guess, the hotter under the collar I got. Pretty soon I was doing a little hollering and she was off upstairs to do some big-time sulking. I was never much good in the tact department, was I? But you wouldn't have sulked. Remember the night we had Lord and Lady Savile to dinner and you made her laugh so hard she got the hiccups and we had to put a bag over her head?

Well, you go apologize to Belle, I'll go apologize to Heidi and everybody'll be friends again.

29

And stop feeling sorry for yourself. You've got everything a woman could want, including all my love.

Jake

Dear Mr. Breen,

Miss Ross wanted me to tell you how sorry she was about your fire. Luckily nothing more important than her picture burned up.

Enclosed find another. Any member of Miss Ross's fan club is entitled to seconds.

Belle Goldman
Secretary to Miss Ross

Sally Ross

Thursday the 6th.

Dear Jake,

Nice try. You always were the best liar in L.A., and that's no mean accomplishment. But your letter could have been written by Disney for all the truth there was in it. Facts are facts, darling. Fifty is fifty and even tortoises have other tortoises. What I do have, however, is an absolutely uncanny gift for being in the wrong place at the wrong time. What else would explain why, in the midst of this downer, I went to see Gwen in *Chicago?* In the middle of the show she has the line "To tell you the truth, I'm older than I ever intended to be." Thank the Lord I went with Hal, so I had a friend to carry me out. Darling, what you wrote about that first little cloud over your honeymoon cottage has started me thinking about our own honeymoon. You're absolutely right. I wouldn't have sulked. I would have sent you to the hospital with a concussion. So count your blessings. It could be you've finally lucked in. Bring Gretel some flowers and don't be an insensitive old goat. No woman talks in front of Robert Redford. Not if she has one drop of estrogen in her body.

Speaking of which, why didn't you ever make me pregnant? Don't answer, I know.

Love from Lady Methuselah.

Sal

32

March 8th, 1976

Dear Ms. Goldman,

I couldn't possibly allow your very snide letter to go unanswered. You may feel that because you have the good fortune to be Sally Ross's secretary, that allows you to be offhand with people, but it certainly does not.

For your information, I am not, nor do I have any intention of becoming a member of anyone's "fan club." Not even for someone as stellar as Sally. I am not one of those silly "little" people as you so smugly insinuated.

Moreover, your reference to Sally's picture as unimportant is, I think, a breach of loyalty. Anyone as wonderful as Sally is entitled to only the purest devotion from her employees. Or would it be fair turnabout to say "servants"?

Douglas Breen
780 West 71st Street
New York City

Dear Mr. Breen,

Are you for real? Listen, I hear Ethel Merman loves to send out pictures. Bother her for a while and give us a rest.

Belle Goldman
Lady-in-Waiting

March 13th, 1976

Dear Sally,

The last thing I would want to do is trouble you. I know what your schedule must be like nowadays and I also know that a creative personage must be left in repose in her ivory tower to sculpt her masterpiece—in this case, your portrayal in *So I Bit Him*. But the enclosed letter I received from your secretary must not go unattended, for your sake. What, I fear, is this person doing to your reputation? I'm quite sure you know nothing about it. The fact is this: I merely requested a picture of you as I have done many times in the past without incident. Suddenly, to be faced with this kind of vituperation, this unnecessary rudeness on her part, is most alarming. For as we know, an employee is a reflection of her employer.

I fear your secretary needs a sharp talking to and a firm reprimand. Doesn't she know that the relationship between a star, such as yourself, and a true fan, such as myself, is sacrosanct?

Again, I regret deeply involving you and would not have done so were there any other way.

Rehearsals for *So I Bit Him* should start soon, according to the "trades." Best of luck, as if you needed it!

Your greatest fan,

Douglas Breen
780 West 71st Street
New York City

35

Sal:

Your grey shoes have had it. Wear the white ones I left
out. Bret said if you don't call him he's going to trade you
in for two ingenues and a trained myna bird. Also, you split
the seam in the seat of your black pants suit. Again. If
you're looking for your snack tonight, try the vegetable
crisper. I'm taking all the Sara Lee home with me. We're
beginning to spend a little too much money on needles and
thread around here. Incidentally, you're on *The Late Show*
tonight. The one where you and Peter Lawford out-cute
each other. Myself, I plan on missing it. Oh, I took your advice and I didn't answer the creep. Only one thing. What
the hell does sacrosanct mean? See you in the morning.

Belle

Also, try not to leave your shoes right in front of the front
door, huh? Some of us who don't focus so well at nine in
the morning could live without an obstacle course.

Sally Ross

Belle,

Got in at dawn's early, so if you fall over my shoes please land quietly. First rehearsal at twelve. Get me up by ten-thirty even if you have to set fire to the bed. I'll need at least an hour to pull myself together for my grand entrance. Also, see if you can locate my feather boa. Hell, if I'm going to do it, I may as well go all the way.

Ha ha on you. You forget the Nestle's chocolate bits in the pantry.

Fatso

Dear Sally,

Just a note to inquire as to whether you had that "little talk" with your secretary yet. Sally, I know what a loving person you are, but sometimes it is a mistake to be too soft with subordinates. They take dreadful advantage. An example in question. At the record shop where I work (temporarily, I assure you, for I do have my "plans") there is a young girl recently hired. Sally, believe me when I tell you she is not the brightest person in the world. It adds painfully to my already busy day to have to explain things to her endlessly and "bail her out." Yesterday, she asked our manager (an ogre) if she might extend her lunch hour to have her hair done. Why is it that some women expect that their personal problems can be put upon the shoulders of their employers? Not to mention those "monthly difficulties," if you know what I mean. At any rate, she arrived back at the shop after three in the afternoon! I was harassed beyond belief, having to do not only my own work, but hers as well! And when I brought this sad state of affairs to her attention, she was rude into the bargain!

You see what a mistake it is to be too human when dealing with people whose only interest is themselves. Have that talk with your secretary. You owe it to yourself, and to those who love you. As I do.

Your greatest fan,

Douglas Breen
780 West 71st Street
New York City

BELLE GOLDMAN

Dear Sal,

Good work, you found me. But I am hiding in the back of the cupboard because I have four billion calories in me and I am for the guests Friday night, not for you. Belle said if you eat me on one of your midnight orgies, the next part you will be offered is the lead in the life story of the Goodyear blimp. She says you should eat my friend, the carrot. It's in the vegetable crisper. She also said she will break both your thumbs if I'm not here in the morning.

Sara Lee

P.S. How do you like the stationery? I figured if you could use the good stuff to leave me notes, the least I could do is the same.

Dear Sally,

I hope yesterday's letter gave you the "courage" to put your secretary in her well deserved place. Did I mention seeing you in *Miss Connie Smith* the other night? Oh Sally, you were enchanting! Of course, Peter Lawford should have thanked his lucky stars to be cast opposite that explosion of adorableness that was you! (Though he is, to give credit where credit is due, exceptionally handsome. I, too, am told I am handsome—not to toot my own horn or anything.)

Sally, I'd dearly love to pick up a bit of "insider's knowledge." From my collection of *Photoplay* magazines, which is considered by experts to be of some value, I understand that you and Peter Lawford were once an "item." Is it true or mere studio hogwash?

Please let me know. Love from

Your greatest fan,

Douglas Breen
780 West 71st Street
New York City

Sally Ross

Dear Belle,

Welcome to the refrigerator. I am a grapefruit. You may eat me. I am also the exact shape of your ass, so watch who you leave notes to. In case you haven't passed a mirror recently, you ain't no Audrey Hepburn yourself.

Madame Arbuckle

Dear Sally,

Well, just time for a few lines before I catch my bus to the record "shoppe."

Life is so tedious at the moment. Thank the Lord that the summer is on its way and vacation time draws nigh. I don't know if I've mentioned it, but I'm on a bit of a diet lately. Must get in shape for the beach! Not that I'm fat. Far from it, Sally. If I do say so myself, my body is in excellent shape—lean and muscular, with biceps and pectorals well defined. But enough about my shall we say "physical attributes." Someday, when we meet, you can judge for yourself!

That girl at the shop continues to be a thorn in my side. Yesterday she told the manager I was looking up her skirt when she climbed up to get records from the top shelf. Sally, I promise you, it's simply not true! It's a case of what she'd like me to do, if you ask me. From the moment she started at the shop, I could tell she found me attractive. No, Sally, I'm not being self-congratulatory. I have been told all my life that I'm unusually good looking. I'm merely repeating what others have said. I have bright blue eyes, a clear complexion, a good body (I already mentioned that!) and a strong, straight nose. She, on the other hand, has none of these attributes and dreadful posture to boot! So she can just forget any smarmy ideas she may have conjured up concerning her and me!

Must run for now. Will write tomorrow and that's a
promise!

Love,

Douglas
780 West 71st Street
New York City

P.S. I'm awaiting the "scoop" about you and Peter
Lawford!

BELLE GOLDMAN

3/25

Dear Bess,

How do you like the stationery? A gift from Sal. You know how much it cost? A buck a letter. Honest, I saw the bill. Now you know how the other half lives.

Thanks for the pictures of the kids. My nephew's getting to be quite a guy. Tell him if he smokes pot again his old aunt'll come out there and pin his ears back.

Sorry about Lennie's sciatica, but I know what you're going through with his complaining. Sal hasn't stopped in a couple of weeks. Her new show is a killer. Some nights she comes in so grey around the edges she worries me. I think I've got a lot of Mama in me. Remember how she used to yell at us when we whined? That's how I am with Sal. I wish to hell she'd get a fella already. Or a poodle or something.

You want to read something nutty? I'm enclosing a letter from one of Sal's fans, the one I wrote you about. Now he's telling her how good-looking he is. Maybe we ought to ask him for a picture. Well, it takes all kinds.

Tell Greg not to smoke pot. It leads to other things.

Love to your gang,
Belle

44

BELLE GOLDMAN

3/25

Dear Greg,

What's this I hear about your smoking pot? What the hell are you doing that for? At your age, life should be enough to get you high. Stop looking for ways to kill yourself. If you stop with the showing off, I'll take you to Sally's opening night party. Deal?

Aunt Belle

P.S. Speaking of showing off, how do you like the Tiffany stationery?

45

CONTINENTAL STUDIOS

Mar. 25, 1976

Dear Sal:

I've got a few minutes between conferences and it was either take a walk around the lot now that we've finally got a cloudy day or write my favorite ex. You won. Everything is fine at home these days. Heidi's taking a class in gourmet cookery, so call your broker and buy Alka-Seltzer.

I've been trying to peddle Franklin the idea of doing a remake of *Camille*, but every time I mention it he just sits there and nods at me like I'm out of my mind. Maybe he's right.

Listen, get the show on fast and we'll buy the film rights. Then you come out here and do the movie and we'll have ourselves a time. I could use one about now. Between Franklin's nodding and Heidi's cooking, my ulcer's back in town.

You're young, you're beautiful, you're terrific. But, then, what do I know? I'm the idiot who wants to do *Camille*.

Love,

Jake

Dear Sally,

Forgive me for not writing but the last few days have been murder!

Well, I finally had it out with the new girl at the shop. What a bitch! The straw that broke the proverbial camel's back came the other day when I asked her to get down a Stevie Wonder album for a customer and she told me to get it myself! What nerve. I immediately stormed up to our manager and laid the whole mess in his lap. Now, here's the shocking part. He told me to leave her alone! That's right, he completely took her side, although I've been working at the shop for more than six months and she's brand new!

Sally, I don't like to conjecture without knowing the full facts, but does it sound to you like he and she are more than employer-employee, if you know what I mean? It would certainly explain a lot of things.

How wondrous it must be to be a star and above the niggling pettiness of shopgirls. Though, of course, your life is not without its problems. Speaking of which, what did your secretary say when you informed her of the proper behavior toward your correspondents? I hope she was properly contrite, but these menials do have their way of turning everything around so that they end up blameless, don't they?

Now, you really must take time from your busy schedule to drop me just a line. I'm still dying to know about you and Peter Lawford. You can tell me, Sally. I

47

wouldn't betray a confidence from you for all the "tea in China." After all, I do love you, you know.

As always,

Douglas
780 West 71st Street
New York City

Sally Ross

Darling Jake,

It's a marvelous idea and if Franklin doesn't see it, it's because his brains are located slightly to the left of his prostate. Don't you dare say another self-effacing word about yourself to me. I was the girl who was there when you pulled Paramount out of the pits, remember?

Are you or are you not drinking milk before meals like you're supposed to, dummy?

But enough about you. On to my favorite topic, me. Today we started blocking out "My Time." It's a kind of "Don't Piss on My Parade" number where I come out and chew up half the proscenium arch from sheer determination. In it, I'm transformed from a dowdy housefrau into a liberated creature complete with cross-your-heart-bra and feathers. Lord, Jake, why do costume designers always want to bury me in feathers? Do I look like a chicken?

So, what has Riggs (or as we kids call him, Tinker Bell) got up his size two sleeve for the number? (I finally convinced him that cartwheels and splits are inappropriate for a hundred and two year old woman.) I spin. That's right, I come out spinning like a top. God forbid I should walk downstage like a normal person. God forbid I should sweep on. God forbid I'm getting too Jewish for words. I guess it was all those years with you, my nice Jewish Prince. Anyway, Tinker Bell wants me to come on spinning and continue spinning all the way downstage and unless they put a net up, right into the orchestra pit. We tried it for a couple of hours, and all I can say is I feel like I just crossed the Atlantic in a gale. What is that midget trying to do, kill me? I ask you, Jake, do you want to see some old bag in feathers spin around like a demented parrot? Whatever happened to glamour? Why is Angela permitted to insinuate herself down a staircase? Why is Betty carried on in something long and slinky? Hell, even Hermione Gingold got wheeled on in a wheelchair, and I've got to come out spitting sweat and feathers?! Are you sure Helen Hayes started this way?

I'm glad all is beautiful between you and Snow White again. It gives us octogenarians hope to know one of us made it. Just be nice, Jake, and don't let your bossy side take over. It ain't your best side, you know.

All in all though, you're not so bad, or why would I still love you?

                                              Your Gal Sal

P.S. Milk!

March 29th, 1976

Dear Sally,

What an incorrigible correspondent you are!

Just kidding, Sally. You are as you have always been, the dearest, sweetest, most heavenly creature in all the world. But Sally, ages have gone by since I asked about you and Peter Lawford, and still no reply! I do need word from you now in my hour of travail. Things at the shop are worse than ever. That girl should be slapped silly. She has taken to saying cruel and untrue things about me behind my back! You of all people know how damaging groundless gossip can be, and the things this snippet says! Unnatural and vicious accusations! All I can say is, she'd better watch her barbed tongue because life has a way of bringing its own comeuppances to those who have nothing better to do than slander their betters.

But enough of me. I read in *The Post* that *So I Bit Him* looks like a sure-fire hit. Of course it will be. Doesn't it have the greatest, the most resplendent, the most thrilling star in the world in it? You know to whom I refer. Despite the fact that she is far from a dutiful correspondent (still kidding). But I would love to hear from you. Take a moment out. For me.

The one who adores you,

Douglas
780 West 71st Street
New York City

March 30th, 1976

Dear Sally,

Still no letter from you!

Things at the record shop are far from satisfactory. If you only knew how much a line from you would mean to me. Soon, dear Sally. Things are not well.

Love,

Douglas
780 West 71st Street
New York City

BELLE GOLDMAN

4/4

Dear Mr. Breen,

I'm sorry but Miss Ross's schedule at the moment does not permit her to answer fan mail in person.

Belle Goldman

April 7th, 1976

Dear Sally,

Again the intervention of your secretary!

Sally, clearly your little talk with her did no good and
a threat of dismissal would be more appropriate. She
flaunts me with snide references to fan clubs and fan letters. Yes, Sally, I am certainly your greatest fan, but I am
much more than that. I am a friend. Someone you can
turn to in times of distress. Someone who will always be
there for you, in any way you want me. I mean that, Sally.
I can be the closest friend you ever had. Your confidant.
And yes, if you so desired, even your lover. It has taken me
a long time to say this but it is true, Sally. And believe me,
I have all the necessary "equipment" to make you very,
very happy. Both in body and in mind.

Explain to that woman who works for you that she is
not to treat me in such an offhand way. Who knows, someday I might be her employer as well!

More love than I can say,

Douglas
780 West 71st Street
New York City

BELLE GOLDMAN

Dear Mr. Breen,

All right, enough's enough. I haven't bothered Miss Ross with your latest letters, but now you're getting out of hand. No one here is interested in your "equipment" and the postal authorities frown on that kind of offer going through the mails. So just suppose you quit writing.

Belle Goldman

Dear Sally,

What a fool I've been!

Now I understand all too clearly why I haven't heard from you. Your secretary as much as admitted to me that she's been destroying my letters to you!

Sally, you must dismiss her at once. It is clear to me that she wants no one to get close to you, lest her position as your secretary be endangered. But *why?* There is more here than meets the eye, Sally, that much I know. Have you checked your jewelry lately? Perhaps a visit to your bank might not be altogether unrevealing. I know the thought of embezzlement is distasteful to say the least, but Sally, you must face facts. Clearly the woman is not to be trusted. To tamper with your correspondence, to prevent letters from reaching you, surely this is only an indication of what this creature might be capable of doing!

I worry for you, my darling. There is nothing I wouldn't do for you, you must believe that. When I think of you, at the mercy of that conniving woman, I shudder!

What I'm going to say now is disturbing, but no stone should be left unturned. Sally, has it occurred to you that that woman might have lesbian tendencies and that is the reason she stands between us? You must exercise utmost caution, Sally. Never dress or undress in front of her. Your undergarments should be laundered when she is out, lest the sight of them arouse her. You must be careful not to use profanities in her presence, as these can also stimulate the imagination.

I know whereof I speak, Sally. I have also had experience with the degenerates of this world. It was in college that my first awakening to this secret world took place. I was in the dormitory shower when another student came in. He loitered at the sink while I finished my shower, but out of the corner of my eye I could see him staring in the mirror, watching my reflection. Watching for a glimpse of my manhood! Needless to say, I outsmarted him. I wrapped myself in my towel while still in the shower to avert his gaze. But I did notice him, weeks afterward, continuing to eye me "up and down." One of the reasons I left college was to avoid any further confrontation with his type. They're everywhere, Sally. Homosexuals have wormed their way into virtually every field of endeavor, and most disturbingly, into politics itself! They are one reason our country is in the sad state it's in. The degenerate mind cannot hope to cope with the complex problems of our society, and yet they find themselves in positions of power! I am not in favor of purges in any society, Sally, but something must be done and soon. Do you realize how much of your tax dollar goes to keeping up homosexual front organizations? And of course the mass media has long since been in the hands of the homosexual.

But enough of my political outburst. We must turn our minds to what can be done for you, to protect you from that woman. I understand that you might be frightened to dismiss her, fearing retaliation. If I were there with you, could you find the courage? No one will hurt you while I'm near, you know that.

I dare not send this letter to your home, in case SHE gets her hands on it. Instead, I will send it to the theater. I will not sign my last name nor my address, just to be on the safe side. You know where you can reach me—the same address you sent your photograph to.

We must talk, Sally. We can devise a plan of action if we work together. After all, there is that old adage. The one that goes *Love conquers all.*

Douglas

CONTINENTAL STUDIOS

April 13, 1976

Dear Sal:

I took a poll at the commissary over lunch. Jack Slattery, Dustin Hoffman and Jane Garth voted yes, they'd love to see you spinning around in feathers. Sidney Lumet and Chuck Wilton said they'd rather see you spinning without the feathers. And Joan Blondell said she'd just love to see you. So be a good girl and do what you're told.

Love,

Jake

P.S. There's no such thing as too Jewish.

LILYAN PETERS

April 12

Dear Sal—

Had dinner tonight with Carol and Joe and Harvey Korman after the taping of their show, and the talk came round to you. Everyone wished you were there to keep us laughing. Carol's cut her hair again, Joe looks gorgeous all grey, and Harvey Korman flirted with me, bless his heart. The grapevine is saying nasty things about your new show, but of course it's too early to tell, isn't it? And if anybody can turn dross into gold, you can. Just remember all the tricks you stole from me. Joe asked if I'd like to do a guest shot on their show, but I don't know. I can't sing, my dancing is abysmal and I learned my sense of comedy from Lee Strasberg, so what would I do? Just stand there and let everyone marvel that I don't look worse than I do? I think I'll pass. Well, dear, good luck with the show and drop me a line when you get a chance.

Love,

Lil

P.S. Had to bury my old Rolls-Royce last week. It was like the passing of an old friend. Thank the Lord diamonds don't wear out.

0

Sally Ross

Dear Lil,

Don't be a dope—do the show. Joe won't let you look bad. And frankly, nobody cares how you sing or dance. You've still got the old studio aura and that's what they'll tune in to see. Just wear a lot of sequins and stick out your front.

Whaddya mean tricks I stole from you?! You bitch. May I remind you it was yours truly who got you through that musical number in *Stepping Out*? There's no gratitude in this world. At least not among us grand dames.

Unfortunately, it's not too early to tell. *So I Bit Him* is going to add the faint aroma of camel dung to the Times Square air. But maybe they'll pull a rabbit out of the hat yet. If not, is this grand dame's face gonna be red.

Do the guest spot, tell Carol to stop cutting her hair (she'll be down to the scalp soon), give her and Joe my love and keep a little for yourself, you bitch I stole all those tricks from.

Sal

P.S. When my first Balenciaga rotted away, Jake and I held a funeral in the back yard, so I know how you feel about the car.

Dear Sally,

Things are worse than I feared!

I don't mean to frighten you, but you must be armed with the truth so that you will know what you are up against.

I decided not to mail the letter, but to bring it to the theater personally on my lunch hour and, in that way, to make absolutely sure it did not go astray, as I fear so many of my letters have in the past.

I went back to the stage entrance and let myself in. A wondrous digression! Standing there in the darkened backstage area, I heard that dulcet, thrilling voice I've come to know and love over the years. Yours! Sally, you cannot know how much it meant to me to realize we were but a few feet apart. You, singing in that world-famous and adored voice, me, with a letter meant for your eyes alone! It was our first shared moment—our first rendezvous, if you will. I was thrilled.

But then it happened.

A woman, middle aged, grey of hair, in a blue and white checked suit of nondescript and unfashionable style came in the stage door behind me and curtly brushed by me. She went up to a man seated at a desk and they chatted for a moment. I stood back, listening. I don't know exactly why I felt it would be wisest not to make my presence known, but thank the Lord Above I did! (Sometimes fate works its miracles in strange ways, does it not?)

He addressed her as *Belle!*

Yes, it was her. *That* woman! I watched and listened, and then it happened, Sally. The tell-tale clue that fate intended me to see! He handed to her mail intended for your eyes alone! Do you understand the full implications of that? Whatever her game, whatever her plan of action against you, she is not in it alone! There are others assisting and abetting her. Perhaps carefully planted, as that man in the theater was. As she was in your home. There may be others in the homes of your friends. Who knows the full extent of this treachery?

I left the theater quickly, shaken to the core. Sally, my dear, I dare not send my letters to you, lest they find out the extent of our knowledge of their nefarious activities. No place is safe to mail these letters—neither the theater nor your residence.

But Sally, I will continue to write. I will not forsake you. Somehow you must know that my thoughts continue to "wend your way," although for the moment I must keep these letters in trust for you. Soon enough, my Sally, I will find a way to get them to you. And to defend you against those who would do you harm.

I love you, but of course you know that already. Trust me. *I will be near.*

Douglas

Angel Jake,

Well, Nirvana is here. A day off. And what better way to spend it than writing to my wonderful, dirty old man. (How is Goldilocks?)

Also, darling, I need advice. I considered Dear Abby, but then I remembered there you are, sitting behind your desk at Continental with nothing better to do than listen to the problems of your own Auntie Mame, so here goes.

I'll make a scenario of it, so you'll feel right at home. Fade in. Gorgeous star, early forties (Listen, it's my scenario!), sneaks out of rehearsals and across the street to a little coffee shop because, darling, five more minutes with our infant composer and I really would look my age. Try to convince a genius that mere mortals need to come up for air between quadrupal internal rhymes. Honestly, Jake, he's got me sounding like the verymodelofamodernmajorgeneral! Belle has to iron out my tongue when I get home. But enough of background, back to the scenario.

Close-up of the absolutely radiant but tired actress sitting in the coffee shop over a little bouillon, staring out the window, wondering why she who has everything should feel, well, somewhat less than ecstatic about her life. Camera pans from ravishing actress to back booth. Close-up of absolutely beautiful young man, giving actress the sweetest smile you ever saw. Oh, Jake, talk about your blue eyes. Talk about your nonexistent waistline. Talk about your two dots for a nose! Medium shot. Breathtaking young man and stunning slightly older woman are sitting at the same table, chatting amiably. Gorgeous young man is so interested in, so sensitive to and so sympathetic with stunning ever-so-slightly older woman it could break your heart. Oh, Jake, it was like looking into the eyes of a cocker spaniel. I thought he was going to lick my face any minute.

Now, unfortunately, we cut to stunning actress galloping across the street, with suitable regality, back to Mr. Mozart. But I looked over my shoulder, and there he was, staring out the coffee shop window at me, looking sweet and dear and sexy as all get out.

Well, that little encounter made my day. I even let our composer convince me I could do a chorus and a half between breaths.

Now, darling, the plot thickens. Fade in on same coffee shop, next day, after rehearsal is over. Ravishing barely forty-year-old actress, costume designer (that man knows from nothing but red. Me, the chorus, even my leading man. Opening night's going to look like a blood bath!) and a few gypsies have decided to go to Joe Allen's and say nasty things about Riggs. (He's actually rather sweet, in a way.) We're walking down the street, attracting attention like mad because Miriam the gypsy dresses straight out of *Barry Lyndon*, and we pass the coffee shop. Who should be there, two little dots pressed up against the glass but the breathtaking young man! He waves and smiles, I smile, I tell the others to wait a moment and I go inside to ask him if he'd like to join us. He says he'd rather have me to himself. HE'D RATHER HAVE ME TO HIMSELF!

Thirty-six-year-old actress goes into swoon and sends the others off to Joe's alone.

Vaseline on the camera lens for the next scene. We sit over coffee and I pour out my heart to him. I complain about Riggs's fetish for gymnastics, I complain about Hollywood, I complain about people who complain, everything. And all the while those gorgeous blue eyes stare and sympathize and practically eat me up. Honestly, Jake, nobody since you has had such endurance for listening to my egomania. Finally even I had enough of the sound of my voice and we just sat there over coffee, smiling and looking, and I got to feeling so young I passed puberty going the wrong way. The worst of it is he was there the next day, too. Just hoping I'd show up. And I did, hoping he would.

What's happening to me, Jake? I was never the kind to have entanglements with young men, was I? (Roger What's-His-Name doesn't count. He was not young, merely stupid.)

But now I find myself thinking about him throughout rehearsal, just waiting to get back to that greasy spoon and bathe in those eyes.

There's something so sweetly strange about him. I know nothing about him, really. (Who has a chance to talk with me around?) But he smiles as if he has a secret—a beautiful, wonderful secret.

Oh Jake, has it really come to this? Getting crushes on young men in coffee shops? I don't care. I've felt so rotten lately, so used up, and now, for the last few days at least, I've felt so good. So hopeful. Is that wrong? I've had more in my life than ninety per cent of the world and if all that hasn't made me happy, shouldn't I try anything that does? So what if Rona Barrett and the girls have a field day.

Of course Belle thinks the whole thing is ludicrous, but Belle can afford to be normal. She lost her husband the fair way, to disease. I lost mine to show business. (Not your career, darling. Mine. I know what a fool I was.)

So, whaddya think, Abby? Does the bitch goddess stand a chance with the innocent blue-eyed young prince? How does it work with you and Bo-Peep? But of course, older men are allowed to fall in love with younger women. Must write Gloria Steinem and see if we can't get equal pay for equal putout.

I told him I'd see him there tomorrow.

Should I? Oh please say yes, Jake. Say whatever you need to get by is aces with me. And be just a little jealous, darling, in a vestigial way, for my sake.

Why don't you and Heidi have a child? A son, Jake. Think of it!

Lord, I sound like Norman Vincent Peale.

Love,

Y.G.S.

P.S. Milk!

Dear Sally,

I have begun.

Soon, my darling, all will be revealed to you and then you will know that you are not alone and at the mercy of foes. You have me, Sally, and all is in *capable* hands!

If I could but tell you how capable these loving hands are, and to what extent they have gone in the past to protect those I love, and to what extent they would go in the future to protect you! I am not a person who is easily manipulated. It has been tried in the past and those who have tried it have learned through "sad" experience that I am not to be toyed with.

An example in point:

A certain tradesman who shall remain nameless once thought to accuse me of petty filchery in his place of business. Sally, I am no thief, neither then nor now. It was clearly a case of the *pot* calling the *kettle* black, as this nameless Jew was notorious in the neighborhood for selling inferior merchandise at exorbitant prices! This vendor approached my parents with his vile lies and they were unmoved by all my protestations of innocence. Some people are fortunate enough to have trusting and loving parents. Alas, such was not the case for me. My father, a taciturn and thoughtless man, paid off the Jew and the entire "situation" was soon forgotten by everyone.

Except me.

Two months later, as fate would have it, the Jew's shop was afflicted by fire and much of his overpriced merchandise damaged beyond salvage. I hope you understand my meaning, Sally, and know that your protector can back up his pledge of action. If only I could send you this letter, how it would help you in your hour of need! But for the moment, we must be cleverer than those who plot against us. These letters must not leave my side.

But on to "lighter" news. I went in search of a proper box to house these epistles, to keep them safe. (Think how tragic it might have been were the letters of the Brownings lost to the world!) I went straightway to Gucci but, pretentious shop that it is, it was closed for the luncheon hour. But I finally found what I was looking for in, of all places, The Godiva Chocolate Shoppe! It's in dark green velvet with leaves, feathers and acorns adorning the top. For the moment, it houses two pounds of chocolates. Would that I could save these morsels for you, but by the time it is safe to give them to you, who knows what state they might be in? And botulism is nothing to "scoff" at. So last night I sat before my television set emptying out the box. There goes my diet!

Meanwhile, on the home front, all goes badly. Friday, the trollop and I had a scene right in front of several customers. The profanities that issued forth from her wretched mouth!

Something must be done on that subject, too. But you must not worry about my problems. Know only that you are safe and I am with you. Closer than you think.

I yearn to make love to you.

Douglas

BREEN
10 Greenwich Drive

April 20.

Dear Douglas,

Last night Mr. Rafferty called your father long distance to discuss your behavior at the store. Douglas, when your father asked Mr. Rafferty to give you that job, it was clearly as a personal favor because of their association in the Masons. You gave us your word that you would *try* this time. Yet Mr. Rafferty told your father that he would have to let you go if there was one more outburst of any kind.

Douglas, you are not taking your future seriously. You're twenty-five now and should be thinking about a career and marriage like other young men of your age.

Your father is losing patience with you, and I must say I agree with him. For your own sake, you must learn to be more tolerant of people and more respectful. It hurt me deeply to hear what you called that young woman at the store. That kind of language was never permitted in our home, and it does no credit to your father or me that you use it outside the home.

Douglas, I want to hear that you are changing and taking things more seriously. You may feel you have many years in which to find yourself, but the years ahead move too quickly to waste. Your father and I do not want to be disappointed in you, Douglas. Please make sure we're not.

Mother

BELLE GOLDMAN

Dear Bess,

Glad to hear Lennie's feeling better. Went to Sid's grave Sunday. I don't know what I'm paying for—they're not keeping it up the way they ought to. It's hard to believe it's been eleven years now since Sid died. It seems like yesterday. Remember how he and Greg used to slug it out? Sid would be so proud of Greg now. A doctor in the family.

Speaking of doctors, I went to my own the other day. Feeling funny lately—listless and nervous. I thought maybe I needed a shot. He says there's nothing wrong with me but I don't know. I'm cranky as hell most of the time and my imagination is starting to work overtime. You know me, I've never been afraid in the streets at night, but the other night I thought someone was following me. Maybe that would be the best thing that could happen to me—a nice single man following me. It sure as hell worked for Sal. She's still seeing that kid, you know. I finally got a glimpse of him at the theater where he was waiting for her. I gotta admit if I was twenty years younger I could go for him myself. Not that it would be appreciated. When Sal introduced us, it was all he could do to smile. Maybe he felt funny in front of me, a kid like that and a woman Sal's age. I don't know, I don't believe in that kind of thing, but I have to admit, Sal hasn't been this happy in a long time. So maybe there's something to it. I just hope when it's over she isn't worse off than before. But then, come to think of it, how could she be worse off than before?

71

All right, enough already. I've got to get my subway home now. Don't want to be here when Sal and her friend arrive. She gets embarrassed, he gets embarrassed and I just feel plain old. Love to your gang,

Belle

Apr. 20, 1976

Dear Sal:

Of course see him. If he makes you happy, I don't care if he's fourteen years old and wears Clearasil. For once in your life, Sal, do what feels good and not what looks good.

You're entitled to so much—to a guy who's smart enough and strong enough to take care of you and love you and give you all the things I wish I had been able to. If this kid can, I'll personally pay his dermatologist's bill.

What do you mean, a *little* jealous? I know I'm not allowed to say this, but I'm a lot jealous. Nobody could ever completely stop loving you, don't you know that? That's why you're a star, not because of your singing.

Franklin just buzzed. Time for another round.

Love,
Jake

P.S. I'm drinking the damn milk!

Sally Ross

Wednesday the 22nd.

Dear Jake,

And precisely what is wrong with my singing?

Thank you, darling, for your letter and your endless understanding and support. You always did give me more than I had any right to ask.

Now, to business. His name is David. He says he's twenty-nine, but I think he's stretching it, which is only fair, since I asked him the other night what he could possibly see in a forty-one-year-old woman like me. God will forgive me, Jake, I know She will. He's there every night after rehearsals waiting to walk me home. (Yes, he carries my script.) God, Jake, it's so flattering and young and embarrassing and marvelous. Yes, and foolish, I know. But the only sensible thing about me is a pair of shoes Belle talked me into buying a year ago that have remained hidden in the back of my closet. (If I ever look down and see them on my feet, I'll know it's time to throw in the towel.)

Chita and Joe asked me to a party Friday night. One of those intimate gatherings of every single person in show business. I want so much to take my little beauty and show him off. And I want so much not to. Oh, Jake, I'm such a coward. One smirk from the maid and I'd be off in a flash to the little girl's room to act like a fool. Which of course I

74

am, for giving a damn what anybody thinks. But then, if I didn't care what people think I'd still be Sally Flaherty with the rhinoid nose from God-forbid Yonkers. I can just see myself with a pocketbook filled with pictures of my grandchildren ("This is Shawn. Gorgeous? This is Susan Anne, who gets straight A's from the nuns.") and a house filled with mar-proof furniture and a husband named Mike who beats me regularly, which might be the best thing for all concerned. What am I talking about? Even in the crib, I recall looking between the slats and recoiling at the lace curtains on the windows. By the time I was five I had saved half the money for my nose job.

The only thing I do miss from those days is the Flaherty. It has a ring to it. Sally Ross sucks persimmons. Sally Flaherty kills a cow.

So, what am I gonna do? Take the beautiful boy or no?

Probably no.

But damn it, I want him there! I'm not robbing the cradle. He's past puberty . . . sort of.

All right, Jake. You win. He comes and that's that.

Seriously, should I ask him? Would you? There's an idea! You call and ask him and let me know what he said. I'm going crazy, as you can see. Sweet Jesus! You don't think he lives with his mother, do you? I wonder who's older, her or me. I wonder if he told her about me. I hope she's this incredible creature with yellow hair and three sets of false eyelashes that she wears at the same time. I hope I never meet her. I hope the Mets win the pennant. Bonkers. Stark raving bonkers.

But I'll tell you something. I like it. It's a hell of a lot more fun going crazy than being very serious about which slipcover material to choose. Love to Heidi. See? I called her Heidi.

Y.G.S.

P.S. There's talk about postponing the out-of-town opening. Doc flew in to see a run-through. The poor darling sat there, his eyes filled with incredulity, and then blurted out something about having to see a man on the coast about recalking his sidings. It's the last we heard from him.

BREEN
10 Greenwich Drive

Dear Douglas,

Just three days ago, after your father's embarrassing conversation with Mr. Rafferty, I wrote asking you to straighten yourself out and to take your responsibilities seriously. Obviously my advice went unattended. Mr. Rafferty just called to tell us he had been forced to let you go.

Douglas, I don't know what to say to you. I had hoped that after all the troubles you've caused us in the past, you would finally be ready to make us proud of you. I see that's not the way it's going to be. Your father is furious with you, as well he should be, and I am more disappointed than I can say.

I don't understand why you refuse to learn from your mistakes. I have never forgotten the trouble you got into in college, but I prayed it was not a pattern that would continue. Now I see that nothing has changed.

Your father insists that he will not help you out this time. You must live within your means whether that be unemployment or a part-time job until you are ready to take on the responsibility of a career and learn how to get along with people.

Douglas, I have only one more thought on the subject. Do you remember the doctor we sent you to after that

77

trouble in school? I know your father felt that a psychiatrist was not necessary, but he did help, didn't he? Do you feel it would help to see someone now? If so, I will speak to your father on your behalf. Clearly something must be done to break this pattern of yours so that someday we can hear good news about you.

Mother

Dear Sally,

Break out the champagne! Call the columnists! Let cheer ring throughout the land! To what do we owe these glad tidings? I am a free man again! Yes, Sally, I finally did it. I bid a not-so-fond "adieu" to the record shop, its manager and his little strumpet!!! It was just too much, Sally, honestly. Too much to bear. Her insults, his lax attitude, the whole "kit and kaboodle." And so I simply quit. On the spot.

The cause of this, my final scene, is as follows: After lunch at a small but not altogether inexpensive Japanese restaurant in the area, I returned to the shop to find that a shipment of new albums was in the process of being unpacked and set out in the bins. So far, so good. But then I was told who was placing the albums in my absence. None other than our "friend," the girl we love to hate, Miss Foul Mouth. Knowing full well that she lacked the necessary "grey matter" to place the albums where they belonged, I hurried to check. Of course, I was right. Jacques Brel under pop males, Simon and Garfunkel re-releases under new groups, and on and on. It was a shambles! There was no way our customers could have hoped to find the album of their choice. Believe me, I have enough to do to keep that place running smoothly without having to forage amid the bins, vainly searching for misplaced records. So naturally I brought this sad state of affairs to our manager's attention. Quietly. Discreetly. With suitable businesslike decorum. But who had tip-toed up behind me and was listening, vulturelike, to my protestations? None other than the perpetrator. (I wonder now whether he had signaled her? A possibility.) At any rate, the despicable urchin actually dared to accuse me of having moved the albums around in the bins, just to make her look bad.

Well, one thing led to another, and once again her foul-mouthed accusations and innuendos were heard ringing out throughout the shop, making customers and sales personnel alike turn and stare.

It was then that our manager made his mistake. Plainly, and in full view of dozens of witnesses, he implied that he, too, suspected me of switching the albums! I was livid! Outraged! It was then that I handed in my resignation from my post of duty, effective *immediately!* I also loudly announced that they could go into bankruptcy for all I cared! Sally, I have worked my fingers to the bone for that shop. I have given more of myself than any other employee. I have kept their business in the "black"—and to be paid back in such a high-handed way! Well, they'll have to manage without you-know-who from now on. I've had it!

Moreover, I am now in the process of retaining an attorney to sue the management for slander and false accusations. I have a reputation to protect and I mean to protect it.

I mean to protect you, too, Sally. Thoughtlessly, I have wandered on about my own problems with no mention of yours. Please forgive me, my darling, but if you only knew what has been done already on your behalf! If you only knew! But I must not, as I've said before, commit this to paper, lest it fall into their hands. Suffice it to know that I am nearer than you think, and soon, very soon, my plan will go into effect!!!

Then, my own dazzling glamorous star, we will be free to express our love, both spiritually and *physically*. You will not be disappointed. That I *know*.

Douglas

Sal—

Couldn't get your red dress in time for tonight. Kill me.
The green one looks better on you anyway. Bret wants to
know if you'll do a *Tonight* show. He can get you on a
plane Sunday night. And listen, would you mind telling
Jackie Coogan not to call me Miss any more? I got a name.
In case you forgot, it's

Belle

Belle,

See? I remembered the name. Please try to remember his. It's David, not Jackie Coogan, Little Lord Fauntleroy or any of your other side-splitting euphemisms. Come on, Belle, be on my side, huh? I know things have been a little strained lately, but give him a chance. He's just shy, not malicious. Please tell Bret no way.

Sal

Sally Ross

Dear Jake,

The last two days have been—how shall I put it?—Armageddon.

But this is not about to become one of my usual letters of Complaint. I shall merely throw my head back and laugh at it all. And that's how they'll find me, laughing, when they come to cart me off to that little sanitarium in the east sixties where all the best psychotics go. You know the one—Schumacher wallpaper, Dior strait jackets, chinoiserie bedpans. I could kill!

First, my own darling Belle. In the following manner—death by stoning with those little round pasta things you put in chicken soup. (I'm being cute. I know they're called matzoh balls. I even remember your mother trying to teach me how to make them.) Belle has taken the most infuriating dislike to David and uses every excuse to drop little insults and hints that his mother is calling. I had no idea she could be so mean. Years with me, no doubt. But it's so unreasonable. I know he hasn't taken to her. It embarrasses him when she finds him here in the morning, but honestly, Jake, if only Belle would put herself out a little instead of the endless snide remarks. She says he's rude to her but when I ask how, Belle says it's not what he says it's the way he says it. Now, I ask you, is that an answer? Why is she doing this? Of all people, why is she adding to my problems? He's just a boy, Jake. He needs to be built up, not put down.

Enough about Belle. I can handle her. Now I'll move on to my real targets—those charming Broadway just-plain-folks who welcomed David into their midst with open scabbards. Yes, I took him to Chita and Joe's party. It was a wee bit of a disaster. Like the Chicago fire, but less frolicsome. Someone should hold an annual Shit of the Year Award because I have some winners. All right, I will. Here are the winners of the Sally Ross Shit of the Year Awards for 1976. The envelopes, please.

To J. Milton Shayne, Broadway director, alcoholic and trisexual about town, a swift kick in the much-used hind-quarters for the bon mot of the evening: "After you're through with him, Sal, can I have him?" Sweet, no?

To Ruth Baxter, actress, chum and cheerleader, a bouquet of twenty-year-old tomatoes in the puss for going on and on about how I was like her big sister in the grand old days at the studio.

To Nitsy whatever her name is (or as I'm told she's known in the trade, Hand Job), a full-scale model of a guillotine and a free trial run for mistaking David for my—I can't even say it.

To Donna Albright, actress, dancer and teeny-bopper, a poisoned lollipop for showing up at that party with that body in that dress. And for parking it next to me.

To the little dancer boy who put the make on David, an exploding dildo.

To the lady from out of town, a morocco-bound copy of

Who's Who to be inserted by her gynecologist for asking David no less than three times, "Are you somebody important?"

And on and on.

Honestly, Jake, it was ghastly, and that's not the worst of it. David got into an argument with some man when I was busy elsewhere and it really did get out of hand for a moment. I thought David would hit him before I could get there and hustle him away. My little angel has a temper. I never did find out what the fracas was about, which is probably just as well.

Oh, Jake, why is life never simple? Why can't prince charmings come in the right size and shape and age? And why did we ever divorce? Whatever I said, I take it back. Now that's done. Your marriage to Heidi is revoked. You are to get on the next plane and get back here. Tomorrow morning, when I wake up, I'll see your face on the pillow next to mine, and you'll be sleeping in your boxer shorts like always, and your socks will be on the floor like always, and you'll have brown breath from those little cigars you smoked the night before, and I'll never be old again or lonely again.

Enough. I'll have myself in tears soon, and everybody knows armored tanks don't cry.

I do love you, though a lot of good it does me. Be especially nice to my replacement, will you? After all, it serves me right. I never would sign a run of the play contract.

Y.G.S.

BREEN
10 Greenwich Drive

April 25

Dear Douglas,

Last night your father and I saw a most disturbing program on television about the gap between a young man and his parents. It got me to thinking about you, and to wondering whether you truly understand how your father and I feel.

If we are overcritical of you and your lifestyle, it is not because we don't care for you. We care very much. But we are parents and parents want nothing but the best for their children. Frequently disappointment is voiced in anger, but you must know that we are on your side. I know that your father is not a verbal man when it comes to expressing his affection and that you've suffered because of this. So have I. But he does care, and so do I. Have you considered my suggestion of seeing someone? There is no shame in seeking help if it is needed, and we do have the money for that purpose.

I await your reply and pray that you will consider my suggestion.

Love,

Mother

April 26th, 1976

Dear Mother,

Thank you so very much for your suggestion and your prayers, but I feel no need for either. Exactly what kind of help are you referring to? I already have an excellent employment counselor and feel confident that any day now I will find the position I've been waiting for. As to my "personal" life, it is showing extraordinary promise at the moment. In your words, Mother, "Nothing But The Best." Must run,

Douglas

87

Apr. 27, 1976

Dear Sal:

I got your letter this morning and loved your awards. Next year, can I submit some nominees? Unfortunately though, most of your winners didn't do anything. You did. By being so damn self-conscious about David. You're a star, honey, and stars can do whatever they want. Let go. There's nothing in you that wouldn't get applause if you'd just let the people see it.

As to having me next to you on that pillow, you forget what I'm like in the mornings. Remember the time you poured the coffee in my bath? That wasn't because I was such a charmer.

Tonight Heidi and I are going on, of all things, a camping trip. Don't ask. Who knows, it might be fun. Take care of my favorite girl and stop caring what people think. I think you're perfect and that's a consensus.

Jake

BELLE GOLDMAN

Dear Bess,

Got the scarf—it's a beauty. You got the talent in the family, all right, and I got the temper. Thanks a million for knitting it.

Things around here have been moving at a swift pace. Straight down. I wrote you about Sal's little friend? Well, now he's here in the A.M.'s too. Don't start in, Bess. Sal's a grown woman and sex, despite what they think out there in St. Louis, is not dirty. Unless you do it very well. Evidently he does, because Sal's nuts about him. But what a shmuck he is! (Also don't start in on my cursing because at my age it would be easier to give up cigarettes.) The other morning he comes into the kitchen when I'm making Sal coffee and he starts in. A touch of cinnamon in her coffee, like in Paris. Just a suggestion, mind you. Maybe a little shredded chocolate, like in Switzerland. Or what about anisette! For crying out loud, I'm trying to get the goddamn water to boil, open the mail and get her out in time, and Donnie Osmond is giving with the cook's tour!

Lately, Sal's been some sweet pain in the ass, too. Much as I love her, I think maybe I ought to take an early vacation this year and leave her and lover boy alone to decide what kind of coffee they want. Why couldn't she pick out a nice guy her own age? Somebody with a head on his shoulders and a job that would get him out of here early. Speaking of which, she gives him money. I know I shouldn't tell you, but it burns me up so I can't keep my trap shut. The other night, they were on their way out to dinner and I saw Sal slip him a couple of bills. He pocketed them in the time it takes a snake's tongue to slap back in place. Nice, huh? That's the kind of thing we got going on here these days.

Also, he goes through her papers. I caught him. He said it was all so interesting he couldn't resist. Goddamn little snoop. What's he looking for? Loose change? I tell you, Bess, I hope I never get to the point where all I want out of life is a man, any man. Thank God for Sid. Once you've had a winner, you're not interested in also-rans.

Speaking of creeps, something weird happened the other night. I got followed home from the subway. It was dark and I couldn't see him, but he stayed behind me for a couple of blocks. Boy, the things this city is coming to. I swear if Sid hadn't bought the house right after we were married, I'd sell it and move to Jersey like everybody else. But after all those years of scrimping and going without to pay it off, it would be like a slap in his face to give it up. Besides, I've got my memories here.

Tell Greg the offer to take him to Sal's opening still holds, if they ever have it. They're talking about canceling the out of town run and staying in town doing previews. If this one doesn't hit, it'll be Sal's first flop, and you know who'll have to pick up the pieces. At least I'm needed. Now, if only we could get rid of lover boy.

Time to hit the subway. Love to your gang,

Belle

ST. BERNADETTE'S HOSPITAL
678 East 198th St., Bronx, N.Y. 10062

April 27

Dear Chuck,

Here I sit in the middle of the emergency room remembering your advice to do my residency at some nice suburban country club hospital instead of this ghetto sideshow. All I can say is Jesus, were you right. I haven't had a decent night's sleep in three days and I haven't gotten laid in weeks. Please God, next year it'll all pay off and I'll join you in private practice and the sixty per cent bracket.

Tonight's been a bitch. TV must be lousy because every nut in town's on the streets. I just took care of a knifing that practically made me puke. Some guy attacked a woman on the subway and really did a job on her. He carved her face up so bad half of her jawbone was exposed, and then he just kept hacking away.

Oh, for the days when the worst problem I'll face is a cataract. Ophthalmology, where is thy sting? Okay, I'm going to try for a nap before the shit hits the fan again. See ya.

Jeff

Sally Ross

Dear Jake,

I tried and tried to call you but they couldn't find you anywhere. The most horrible thing has happened. Belle was attacked and nearly killed last night. God, Jake, it's the worst nightmare. She was on her way home to that jungle she lives in, when she was mugged on the subway platform. I've tried and tried to get her to move in with me but no, she had to live in that damn house of hers. Now she's in the hospital with God knows what injuries and she still isn't conscious. Her doctor wouldn't tell me a thing. It seems you have to be next of kin to get any information in these stinking hospitals. All he said was that she was attacked and that she's sedated. But thank God, she'll be all right. He swore to me she would. I'm calling Paul Gross tomorrow. He's a trustee at Mt. Sinai and will get me in to see her. Or else I'm going up there and rip the building apart, brick by brick.

God, Jake, why would anyone do it? What could she have had on her? A few dollars? Whatever he got, I hope the son-of-a-bitch spends it on an overdose. I hope they find him dead in some alley. I only wish I could do it myself.

Jake, if I haven't reached you by the time you get this letter, please call me immediately, whatever the time here or there. I must talk to you. With Belle gone, there's no one else to turn to. I don't even know where David is. I waited for him after rehearsal but he never showed up. It's just as well. I'm in such a state, you're the only person I could talk to. Please call right away.

Sal

Sally Ross

Thursday the 29th.

Dear Jake,

I got your letter. What a shame to be off somewhere in the wilderness!

They still won't let me in to see Belle, but Paul got on the phone and found out what happened. She was attacked with a knife and cut up pretty badly. Thank God, she will be all right. They were going to put her in a double room after she gets out of intensive care, but I finally convinced her doctor that I was good for the money and he's trying to find her a private. Oh, Jake, this place is so horribly depressing. I don't see how anyone can get well here. I called Paul and tried to get Belle moved to Mt. Sinai, but he said it couldn't be done, not now, at least.

Meanwhile, I don't know what I'm doing. I've spent the last day and a half in that hell hole, just sitting, waiting for some word. Thank Heaven for David. The poor thing doesn't know what to say to ease things for me, but at least he's here now. This afternoon, when her doctor assured me for the millionth time I wouldn't be allowed to see her, I went back to rehearsal. What a business. That old saw about smiling when you're sad left out the real point—that it kills you to do it. Sometimes I think my real feelings, if I've still got any, are buried under so many years of being tough and laughing on the outside that I'll never get back to them. I swear to you, Jake, I sat there in that hospital, a few yards away from my best friend who's lying there mugged, and when people started staring at me, it actually occurred to me to wonder if my make-up was on! What kind of monster could do that?

I feel so guilty. I've been so bitchy to Belle lately and now I can't even get in to see her and tell her I love her and I'm sorry.

Where are you, anyway? Suppose it was me lying there? They couldn't even reach you to tell you. Leave a number, for heaven's sake, don't just run off.

I'm sorry. I'm just going a little crazy. Please call as soon as you can.

Sal

JO COLTON

Dear Sal,

Sylvan and I are so worried about you, after our phone conversation last night. Tried to call this morning but you were out. At the hospital, I suppose. Sal, there really isn't anything you can do there and you sound so terribly distraught. Wouldn't it be better to come out here and stay with us for a few days? Just until you feel better. Or if you like, say the word and I'll come into town. I don't like the idea of your being alone now.

                                                        Jo

Western Union   Telegram

04/29/76 1388

MS SALLY ROSS

941 FIFTH AVENUE

NEW YORK NY

ARRIVING IN NEW YORK SATURDAY AFTER-
NOON AND WILL GO DIRECTLY TO HOSPITAL.
THANK YOU BUT PLAN TO STAY AT BELLE'S
HOUSE. THANK YOU FOR EVERYTHING.

                              BESS ASHER

April 30th, 1976

Manager
Water's Edge Inn
Sag Harbor

Dear Sir:

I should like to reserve your finest suite for the period from
May the twenty-sixth through May the twenty-eighth,
1976.

We require your best accommodations—a separate sitting
room, dressing room and, of course, a private and luxurious
bath.

I will arrange for flowers to be delivered before my guest
and I arrive on Saturday evening. Please see to it that they
are artfully arranged in the sitting room.

We also require on arrival a tray of canapés and a bottle of
champagne, properly chilled. Imported, please.

I enclose my check for one hundred dollars as a deposit.

Please see to it that everything is as it should be. You see,
my guest for the weekend is none other than the international star, Sally Ross, and wherever Sally and I choose to
vacation soon gets the close scrutiny of the very best class of
persons.

I await verification of this reservation.

Sincerely yours,

Douglas Breen
780 West 71st Street
New York City

April 30th, 1976

ARNO Florist
Sag Harbor

Dear Sir:

I shall be a guest at the Water's Edge Inn commencing the twenty-sixth of May, 1976.

My companion and I will be arriving approximately at midnight. I would like delivered in advance of that hour several bouquets of your finest floral creations.

Red roses, I think. Long stemmed. A dozen.

Violets. Several small and artful bunches, appropriately placed in crystal vases, if possible.

A single spray of orchids, placed on the bed table. Not the small green ones one sees in the better floral shops in New York. Pink, or perhaps white. I leave this up to your expertise.

I enclose thirty-five dollars by personal check as deposit for above.

Sincerely yours,

Douglas Breen
780 West 71st Street
New York City

Dear Sally,

Now you know.

And any thoughts you may have had about my sincerity, any doubts as to my ability to protect you must now be gone, washed away by my "tidal wave of love."

My darling. My star. My mate.

It was all so delightfully simple! Those purveyors of popular entertainments would have one believe that a violent act is ugly and brutal. Such is simply not the case! It is beautiful—almost balletic—and it has a sensuousness of its own, not unlike the act of love.

I want to share it all with you.

I arrived at your apartment at approximately four in the afternoon. And a sumptuous afternoon it was! The sunshine dappled the pavements as it "fluttered" through the trees in Central Park. Across the street, your apartment house, majestic and old-world, stood like an old friend welcoming me, saying "I'm glad to see you again, Douglas. Today is the day, is it not?"

I sat on a bench in front of the park and waited. As I sat there, people passed me and I studied their grey and ordinary demeanor. Poor simple little people, frightened and timid. Which of them had the bravura to do what I would do before that day was over? I fondled the knife in my pocket, knowing that it was the instrument by which I was to prove my love, my adoration of you. Don't think me crude, Sally, but sitting there, stroking the knife, it seemed to become, in a poetic and nonlascivious way, my "male organ," erect and strong, waiting only to serve you. I admit, the prospect of serving you did excite me, but that is as it should be, is it not? True love, such as ours, is a thing of the body as much as of the soul, for the body is the instrument of the soul.

As I sat there, an old man made his way up the avenue, straining to push one of those carts that sell hot dogs and beverages. Several children ran up to him and bought his wares and I wondered whether some day it would be our children, dashing in delight to satisfy their cravings. Of course I do understand that it would be extremely difficult for you to juxtapose motherhood and your career, and for that reason I leave the choice completely up to you. I would, of course, be delighted at the prospect of fathering another "little Sally" but never at the risk of interfering with your career. We must be sensible, Sally. You owe your public a great deal. For surely they have "put you where you are," and they do love you. Love of that sort brings its own responsibilities, and we must not be selfish. For we are not ordinary people, free to live our lives with no thought to others. We are, whether it be fortunate or ill, in the "limelight" and must address ourselves to it. This is, of course, premature, but dreams are the "stuff" of which we mortals are made and so I dream on. Of you, my darling.

But I digress.

It was about five o'clock when that woman rounded the corner and went into your building, laden with packages. I recall wondering whether some of those packages were intended for herself rather than you, bought with what was no doubt stolen money or forged charge plates. Even across Fifth Avenue one could see the true nature of her being. The way she walked, so slovenly, so without dignity. Just before she went into the building, she stopped to say something to the doorman. Of course, I was too far away to hear, but there was something about the way they leaned into each other, something clandestine, if you know what I mean. I made a mental note to study him at another time. We cannot be too careful.

Then I returned to my bench and my vigil. I did not have to wait long. Several minutes after six, she came out and turned east at the corner. I followed at a safe distance. On Lexington Avenue she went into the subway. I did likewise. I stood down the platform from her, hiding myself behind a pillar so that she would not see and recognize me. The train came. I entered the same car at its opposite end.

Heaven was on our side, Sally, for the subway car was filled, making it easier for me to view the woman without her noticing my intent stare.

But oh, the people! The stench of those poor pitiable denizens of this world, scurrying home to their little cells to catch but a few hours of sacred rest before entering this sordid train to go back to their meaningless tedious jobs. Thank the Lord Above, Sally, you have never known this kind of life. I thank God for myself that I am soon to be rid of it forever.

I looked around at the people and wondered whether any of them would find relief from their lives as I am soon to find relief from the life others would have me live. But no, the faces were lost and beyond recall. Hopeless humanity, all. At that moment, I truly felt something akin to the pity that certain religious figures are supposed to have felt for the poor masses. I wished them well. I really did.

But my sole responsibility is to you, and I must not

dilute that responsibility with protestations for others. They will have to assume their own responsibilities as best they can. But I do wish them well, Sally. We have so much and they so little.

By now the train was hurtling into the Bronx, having lost many of its inhabitants. I stood with my back toward that woman lest she see me, but in the reflection from the door where I stood, I could see her. She sat dozing, her head occasionally nodding. For a brief moment I almost felt sorry for her, too. But then I remembered the peril she placed you in and all sorrow vanished. I do not know what made her the way she is, but I do know it is not up to us to excuse the villainy of others. We must put an end to it. To understand is not to forgive, it is merely to understand.

The train pulled out of the Crotona Park station and the woman shook off her drowsiness and got up. She stood by the door at one end of the car. I awaited at the other.

At the next station, she got out.

As did I.

With the knife in my jacket pocket, my hand held tight around it, I followed. Several others got off the train, too, but Sally, Heaven was still on our side. The woman chose to exit by means of a staircase at the far end of the platform. Alone. I hurried along behind her. She pushed through a revolving metal gate into a small vestibule that led to a stairway to the street. I pushed through behind her.

I called her name and as she turned, my substitute "male organ" sliced through the air and into her face. And again. It was as if it were happening in slow motion, the upraised knife slowly descending, her body lurching forward and falling to the ground as if through water. I do not know how many times I struck her or where. I only know I myself viewed this happening as if through a dreamlike mist. A ballet of right against wrong. Surely the valiant warriors of the Crusades knew this exhilaration!

When it was over, the calm and peace that follows an act of love descended on me. I went up into the street, walked for several blocks, mounted a bus and started my trip back to reality. All the while I sat on that bus, looking out the window at the passing houses and humanity, I knew that I had experienced an act of love such as few men have ever known.

And all for you, my dearest.

Douglas

P.S. I fear nothing now. I shall mail this letter to your home. If I do not hear from you, I will know that my instincts about your doorman are correct and I shall know what to do.

P.S.#2. A thrilling surprise awaits you, my darling. More about it at another time.

Sally Ross

Dear Jake,

Thank you, darling, for sitting up half the night with me on the phone. You're always there for me when I need you, aren't you? You'd think after all these years you'd tell me to collect my emotional leftovers from your closet and get out of your life, but you don't and I love you for it. I hope Heidi understood.

I saw Belle this afternoon for a few minutes. Jake, half her face is wrapped in bandages and she's so pale! She's being fed intravenously and there's a tube in her nose. When I first saw her, I almost cried. My poor darling Belle. But then, as I sat there, she started to smile. She even called me names when I did cry. There never was anyone like her.

Or you. What have I ever done to deserve both of you?

All my love,
Sal

Dearest Sally,

I have had a dream, and you must know who it was about. You!

In it, I came across you sun-bathing on a stretch of white and deserted beach. (More about the setting at another time!)

You lay there, your face uplifted to the blazing sun, those perfect and world-adored features beneath a coating of some protective balm, the scent of which assailed my waiting nostrils. You wore a modest bathing suit of white and blue stripes and as I stood above you looking down at your voluptuous womanhood, my own manhood stirred within me.

You opened your eyes and looked up at me.

You held your arms up to me, beckoning me closer, your moist lips parted waiting my kiss.

And I gave it to you, my dearest! There on those white sands, the waves at our feet, our lips met and discovered each other! Your hands moved down my yearning body until they reached the center of my manliness and you caressed and stroked it, uttering sighs and moans and flattering innuendos as to its strength and firmness and size. And oh, the size, my darling! Swelled to its utmost by its longing for you!

Then my hands moved across those lovely shoulders and down to your waiting breasts, those firm double fruits from a garden of love. I caressed those ripened fruits and tasted of their sweet nectar. My tongue, moving ever onward, left a moist trail down the goddess body to the secret recesses of its most treasured jewel. I tasted its nectar and you stirred and moaned and told me that there had never been anyone but me and never could be. And beneath me, your body echoed the rise and fall of the waves and I knew that all I had done and all I might do to hold and protect you was but the beginning. That here was the love that we have waited for, alone and unharmed, in an alien world.

That is how it is for us, Sally. Belle Goldman was only the first to feel the wrath of your protector. Fair warning to anyone who dares stand between me and my adored Sally.

I will be there soon, Sally, my darling, to taste of that nectar I hold so dear.

Douglas

CONTINENTAL STUDIOS

May 3, 1976

Dear Sal:

There's no one in the world I'd rather sit up half the night with than you. I just wish it could be for laughs and not because of poor Belle. Give her all my love, will you?

And stop wondering what you've done to deserve us. It's simple. You loved us.

Jake

Sally Ross

Dear Jake,

Either Belle will be entered in the Guinness Book of Records under recuperative powers or I'm getting used to seeing her in that hospital bed, because this morning she looked absolutely marvelous! She's even tougher than I am, and you can't get much tougher than that without growing a horn in the middle of your face. She'll mend, good as new.

Her room is filled with flowers from everyone. Jo and Sylvan drove into town with a bouquet from their own garden. So sweet.

Did I write that Belle's sister is here from St. Louis? She looks so much like Belle, and we carried on like we'd known each other for years. However, profanity does not run in the family. Every time Belle let go with a beauty, Bess blanched and looked apologetically at me. Even in that dreadful place, the three of us had a wonderful time. It was like a sorority pajama party. I felt so good, in fact, that I went back to work this afternoon. Everyone's been marvelous, working around me for the last couple of days, but it's time to get back in harness. In my absence, Riggs, who it turns out is the dearest thing on two feet, even if they are tiny, worked out a new entrance for my feather number. Now I get to rustle instead of pluck them. I actually think it might work.

David. Yes, David. Jake, I don't know. Sometimes I think he's a Godsend and sometimes I think he's a third nostril. We left the hospital the other night and I was so tired, so down I could have crawled into bed with Belle. What did he want to do? To go out to Joe's and have "a few laughs." I explained to him it would take Ronnie Reagan and Gerald Ford both in drag doing the salsa to make me laugh, but he kept on and on about it. I finally gave in, just for one drink. Stephen and Carol Schwartz were there, and we sat with them. Jake, they're about his age and yet they behaved like grown-ups, why couldn't he? He acted so damned silly that it embarrassed the three of us. He went on and on about Paris in the spring and the Boulevard St. Michel and the boring Tuileries and the incredibly tedious Petit Palais. When I finally did get him out of there, at two in the morning (and the old lady had rehearsal the next A.M.) we went home and he started La Grand Pout. It seems I never do anything for him. He spent two days at that hospital for me and we can't spend five minutes somewhere for him. Well, you know me, Jake, patience is my middle name. So I let him have it, right between the gorgeous blue eyes. (Did it ever occur to anyone that blazingly blue eyes may be linked to retardation? Maybe there aren't enough hormones or something to make the color settle down to a nice usual blue.) So he started to cry and I started to feel like Lucrezia Borgia and we made a truce.

I know beggars can't be all that finicky, but I still wish he were you. Speaking of which, why ever did you take Heidi on a *camping* trip? The Jake I knew thought exercise was when you opened a bottle of champagne, and now you're hiking up and down mountains? You're not trying to act the young stud for your child bride, are you? Because believe me, Jake, if she wanted John-Boy, she would've married John-Boy and not my dear, slightly overweight and completely lazy Jake. So stay, little Valentine, stay. But as for me, I must run. Have to take away the dry cleaning or I'll have nothing to wear. Now I see just how much I need Belle. Everything is missing and out of place, the mail is piling up (I only open envelopes from Continental, my darling) and the phone is driving me crazy. Tons of love and gratitude,

Y.G.S.

May 1st, 1976

Dear Mother,

I know Father said that he would not help me and so I shall not ask for that assistance, although at present I find myself in dire financial need. However, I do recall that Grandmother Breen mentioned me in her will. I have never requested that sum hitherto, but now am forced to do so. I understand from a friend, who is a registered attorney, that that inheritance should have come to me four years ago, when I reached the legal age of twenty-one. But I do not wish to "stir up" any family trouble. I only wish what is mine. Please send it on as soon as convenient, as I intend to leave New York for a short period of time on the twenty-sixth of this month and need the cash by that time.

I am pleased to inform you that my plans are now in "full gear" and soon, very soon indeed, you and Father will hear such news of me that you will hardly believe your ears. All disappointments you have alluded to in the past will be replaced by pride and yes, even deep respect. Please send the money with all haste.

Douglas

May 4th, 1976

Dear Sally,

Each morning I rush down to the mailbox, jumping the stairs two at a time in my excitement, filled with a longing that only you can satisfy. But still no letter has come!

Sally, I did expect that after my "action of love" you would have written. No, I am not asking for thanks. True love is given freely, without the need for gratitude. But I did expect some word, some indication that you were pleased, that life had become better for you, since that is why I did the deed. Then, too, my last two letters have gone unanswered. Sally, I do so need a word from you. I know we must be clever. Now there are police to contend with, as well as the others who were in league with your secretary. But no one is watching my apartment. Surely you could find some means of posting a letter without being observed. If you fear writing anything incriminating in it, make no mention of our relationship. A mere cordial note will do. I will be able to read between the lines, and find the love I so long for.

Sally, if you are holding off writing because of my last letter, I can only say that I am truly sorry if it offended you. It was a mere dream and not meant to be crude or salacious. I truly believe that when two people are in love, as we are, their bodies become sacred tools for expressing that most divine of all things, the act of love. I know I am of a generation that has come to understand that sex is not a thing of repugnance, and that you are not of my generation. But Sally, I mean to help free you of those restrictions that were placed upon you as a child. I mean to show

113

you that the joy of love is nothing to be ashamed of. And so, since this is my attitude, I felt no "compunctions" about describing my dream in all its beauteous details.

Please, my darling, do not be affronted at my directness. It was not for lack of respect of you, but for love of you that I wrote.

So please, my love, answer me quickly so that I know all is well. I am beginning to fear another interloper. If such is the case, do not be afraid. I have demonstrated that I know how to deal with your enemies, and my fervor has not decreased. Nor my love.

Douglas

P.S. Glorious surprises await you, my darling. There is so much you do not know. Soon all will be made clear. I love you.

Sally Ross

Friday the 5th.

Dear Jake,

So much news. Belle is practically her old self again. The tube is gone, she's on liquids, and she's absolutely furious at having to be in the hospital. She remembers very little of what happened. Just hearing someone call out, turning and being hit. It's a blessing. It took days for me to erase the picture of what I imagined from my mind. At least she's spared that nightmare. The police were up to see her, but of course she couldn't tell them a thing. It seems the mugger must have panicked, because he ran off without taking Belle's money. They thought perhaps it wasn't a mugger at all, and that Belle might know more than she was saying, but was afraid to tell. They don't know our Belle. The last thing she was afraid of was a caterpillar that crawled onto her baby blanket. Meanwhile she's wreaking havoc on the poor hospital staff and has earned a nickname among them. B.P. It stands for bed pan and I think it has something to do with Belle's nun-like way of putting things. I loved it. So did she, when I told her. You should see her laugh. She puckers out the side of her mouth and goes hoo-hoo so she won't move the stitches. Just to be mean, I've been collecting jokes all week for her. Yesterday she threw a glass of water at me when I told her one.

Your flowers are still gorgeous and the note was the best we've had yet. It got a four hoo-hoo rating. Belle said she'd write you soon.

Now, as to the rest of my so-called life. This afternoon Edgar assembled the company for an announcement. A week from Monday, ready or not, *So I Bit Him* starts previewing! Jake, we were stunned. No one knew what to say. I mean, we're not even sure of how the damn thing ends yet! In the silence that followed, a herd of fire engines passed the theater with their usual racket, and Edgar, without missing a beat, said, "I think they're overreacting." Talk about your signs from above!

But what on earth are we going to do? I spoke to our book writer, whose eyes have had a very strange glaze over them lately, and he said he was trying for an open-ended feeling at curtain, which means that he hasn't a clue. Jake, in the second act of this little nuclear device, my husband leaves me, my son leaves me, even my best friend takes a walk, and how does our writer suggest we resolve it all? I simply stand there center stage, watch them all go, turn to the audience, stick out my brave little chin and say, "They'll be back!" Then into a reprise of "My Turn" in which I prove, beyond a shadow of a doubt, that I am one of the meanest, most uncaring sons-of-bitches in the latter half of this century. Eleanor Roosevelt couldn't have gotten away with it!

Now on to my last topic of complaint—David. David has it in his pretty little head that I'm going to take him on a cruise or something. Poor darling needs to get away. I explained to him that I happen to be in rehearsals for a play that, heaven forbid, starts previews in a week and, moreover, I wouldn't leave Belle alone now. But he'll have none of it. Oh, Jake, I don't know what to do. I know this little fling isn't going to amount to a row of beans, but I do still care for him. I know that soon enough either he'll wake up, take a good look at me and run in horror, or I'll get fed up, but I'm just not ready yet. It feels so wonderful to have someone to come home with at night, instead of sitting in that Jacobean four-poster by my lonely, watching Joe Franklin and doing my needlepoint. I don't think I'm cut out to be that goddamn dainty.

Now I must get to this apartment. There's clothing, shoes, unopened mail and dishes all over the place. The cleaning woman will give notice unless I tidy up a bit.

I love you, don't go on any more camping trips, drink your milk, believe in yourself and button up your overcoat.

Y.G.S.

117

ST. BERNADETTE'S HOSPITAL
678 East 198th St., Bronx, N.Y. 10062

5/5

Dear Bess,

Thanks a million for flying in. It helped a lot to have you here. And just think, we finally got together and you did all the talking. Isn't Sal something? I knew you two would hit it off. She's here all the time, kidding me, annoying me, hollering at me, sticking up for the moron nurses and that shmendrick in white. Speaking of the shmendrick, he laid a little news on me this morning. It looks like I'm going to need a little plastic surgery somewhere down the pike. Well, I was no beauty before. Maybe now's my chance. As long as he's at it, I think I'll ask him for Olivia de Havilland's mouth, and maybe he could tuck up a little here and a little there and I could pass for thirty-nine again. Sal would be furious. She likes to pretend I'm older than she is. It'd serve her right. She takes everybody's side but mine. Including one little number right out of nursing school who thinks you give needles into the bone. Meanwhile, I'm relaxing and getting the star treatment, except for the food. I'd give my right arm for a hot pastrami on rye with mustard and my other arm to be able to eat it. Have one for me, will you, and tell Greg I'm sorry not to be able to take him to Sal's opening night party. I'll take him to the closing night instead.

Love to your gang,

Belle

P.S. Don't mention the plastic surgery to Sal if you talk to her. She'll just start carrying on and be a bigger pain in the ass than she already is.

BREEN
10 Greenwich Drive

May 6

Dear Douglas,

Your mother and I were very upset by the last two letters you sent her, but in the latest one you hurt as well as
upset us. The money your grandmother left was to go toward your education, and that's exactly where it did go. All
of it. If you want, tell your lawyer friend that. As far as
your future plans go, your mother and I wish you the best
but at this moment we're not sure whether or not those
plans concern us.

Dad

May 7, 1976

Dear Sal:

I know what you're going through with David, baby, because I'm going through the same thing with Heidi. She still hasn't warmed up to any of my friends, she sits around the house just waiting for me, she can't understand why I'm late as often as I am and why I drag myself through the door and into bed. And she has a whole new repertoire of ways of getting even, from sulking to crying to lying there like a dead thing. Has it occurred to you how funny it is that we both ended up with people so much younger than ourselves? Just when we ought to have someone who's been through what we've been through and understands. Why the hell can't we just get old without fighting it? Maybe it's because we don't have each other any more. Sometimes, late at night, I go downstairs and make myself a drink (All right, I know I'm not supposed to. Shut up.) and I light a fire and sit in front of it and try to remember what split us up. The damndest thing is, I don't know. I doubt that two people ever wanted a marriage to work more than we did, but I don't understand why it didn't. It sure as hell wasn't that we didn't love each other enough. Tell you what, I'll turn around, you kick me, then you turn around and I'll kick you.

I've got to figure out some way to get Heidi out of the house and into something. Maybe that'll get her off my back. The thing is, I do love her. She's a wonderful girl. But maybe that's it. She's a girl, not a woman, and my days as a boy ended a long time ago.

Incidentally, you were right about the camping trip, but I've always had a thick slice of the idiot in me, haven't I?

Take care of Belle and yourself.

                                                    Jake

Sally Ross

Dear Jake,

Your letter arrived this morning. It's the only one in the mounting pile that I opened. I expect my electricity will be turned off soon unless I tackle the mail, but I'm glad I saw the Continental envelope because your letter troubled me. You know I've always preferred reading between the lines rather than the lines, and what I saw between yours made me both sad and angry. Now, without being asked for it, I shall launch into one of my famous advice to the lovelorn columns. Jake, you've only been married a few months. Don't you remember what we were like the first few months? All those broken dishes and slamming in and out of the car and packing and unpacking?

I just don't understand it. I was always the hothead, you were always the patient one. Now you sound like the boy in *Barefoot in the Park*, all huffy and injured and self-righteous. She's not even thirty yet. She's a baby. What do you expect? Being a wife to a man as important and busy as you are is no easy task, believe me. I've been there. Nobody wants to slave over a hot soufflé to be called at the last minute and told to freeze it. If she feels out of place with your friends, she is. Your friends are all cocktail party monsters, like me, and she's a young goat-milking girl from the mountains. Patience, my darling. Soon enough she'll discover her credit cards and get Purchase Fever and spend her days scurrying in and out of Tiffany's and Giorgio's and not give a rat's ass about when you come home or with whom. Then you'll have just what you want, a genuine L. A. Princess with a permanent tan, like a garter snake, three-inch fingernails and teeth as white as virgin caps. Which is my roundabout way of saying enjoy her vulnerability and her humanness while she's got them and stop acting the injured saint. Besides, my darling, you do have a few minor flaws yourself. Silly little things like taking a woman by the elbow as you walk down the street but always walking a step in front of her, so she has to side-step like a goddamn geisha. Or staring at a person as if you're listening for five minutes and then saying "What? I missed that," because you were looking at her nose and wondering why shiksa noses are shorter than Jewish ones. Or, while I'm on this fun topic, what about your terrific way of *announcing* that it's time to screw, as if the lucky little lady has been sitting around, just champing at the bit? And your best flaw of all. The way you

Belle just called from the hospital. She thinks she remembers that just before she was attacked she heard someone call her name. I don't understand. If someone called her, then they saw the whole thing. Why didn't they call the police? It couldn't have been the man who attacked her, could it? Someone from her neighborhood? I told her to call the police right away and tell them, but she doesn't want to. She says it's a feeling she has and she can't be sure, but I told her if she didn't call them, I would. How could anyone who knew her by name do that to her, and risk getting caught for a few dollars? It doesn't make sense —but then, violence never does. I think I'll head back to the hospital in a little while—Belle sounded upset. The house and the mail can wait. I'll get to them tonight when I get home from Peri's. She's having a small dinner party and I'm going. Sans David. More about that later.

I love you and I wish you would keep your temper, for your own sake. She is your bride, you know.

                                              Y.G.S.

P.S. Incidentally, your best flaw concerns your habit of doing a certain quaint thing while making love. Think hard. Something midway between Masters and Johnson and Krafft-Ebing. Not that I ever minded, God knows.

EDITH PATERSONN
941 FIFTH AVENUE

May 10, 1976

Dear Mr. Stern:

I tried calling you earlier in the day, but was told that you would not return until the late afternoon, and since my husband and I plan to drive to East Hampton soon, I felt a quick note might accomplish my purpose.

Mr. Stern, you are aware that my husband and I have been dissatisfied for some time with The Bradford because of our proximity to Miss Ross. Well, last night, or should I say early this morning, a difficult situation became intolerable.

At approximately two o'clock this morning, Miss Ross started to scream. I do not mean her usual light-hearted revels, but true screaming. Several of the residents on the floor rushed into the hallway to see what was the matter, including my husband. Miss Ross continued to scream, including various profanities, while the gentlemen rang her doorbell and pounded on the door, to see if she was all right.

The next sound we heard had to be the breaking of every dish and glass in her apartment. And more obscenities. At which point, she came to the door and told us all to go away. We went back into our apartments and tried to salvage what little sleep was left.

This morning several of the shareholders got together informally at my apartment to see what might be done. I was asked to contact you. The point is this: if Miss Ross cannot be convinced through polite means to curb her late-night noisemaking, we are quite prepared to take legal action against her. Mr. Thomas Braddley in apartment 11D is an attorney and will represent us in this matter. I will call you on Thursday when my husband and I return from the country. I hope by then you will have spoken to Miss Ross and can assure us of some meaningful progress.

Sincerely yours,

Mrs. Edith Patersonn

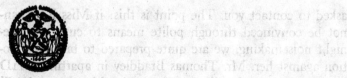

19th Precinct

Stan—

Caplan wants you over at 941 Fifth Avenue, the Ross penthouse, as soon as you get in. Give Anderson whatever you've got left on the Williams case, as he'll be taking it over.

Willy

19th Precinct

Pat,

The Williams files are pretty much up to date but there's a deposition coming in late today from the old lady's lawyer. Welcome to the case and lots of luck. I hope you're as angry at being switched around and pulled off your case as I am. What does Caplan think we are, detectives or secretaries? He's a cocksucker, that one.

Stan

To be posted on bulletin board

TO THE ENTIRE CAST AND CREW OF SO I BIT HIM:

Due to illness, Sally Ross will be unable to attend rehearsals for the next four or five days. The new opening for previews is *MAY 19*. Check the revised rehearsal schedule below for your calls.

Tim

LILYAN PETERS

May 11th, 1976

Dear Sal,

I called Belle at the hospital this afternoon and she told me what happened. My God, what a nightmare! I know the police are doing everything they can, but wouldn't you feel safer out of New York now? To hell with the show, your safety comes first. Why don't you fly out here and stay with me until the police catch him? The servants are here and so am I, so you won't be alone.

I spoke with Jake and he thinks it's a good idea, too. You shouldn't be alone now, Sal. I know what you must be going through. Please consider coming out. It's an awful time to be alone.

Lil

JO COLTON

May 11

Dear Sal,

I don't care what you said on the phone, I think Sylvan and I ought to come in and stay with you. Please let us, Sal. We've been friends for fifteen years and that does entitle us to share your bad times as well as your good. And stop taking Valium or stop drinking. Both together are stupid and dangerous. This will pass, Sal. They'll catch him.

All my love,
Jo

JO COLTON

May 11

Dear Sal,

Already mailed the first letter but thought of something else. If you don't want us to come in, why not come out to the island and stay with us? Belle is safe where she is and you'd be safe here. How about it?

All my love,

Jo

Sally Ross

Thursday the 11th.

Dear Jake,

Thank you for what you said on the phone this morning, but you were wrong. I *am* responsible for what happened to Belle. I can't bear it, but it's true. When I told her about the letters, she sat up in her bed and stretched her arms out to me. I cried like that, with her holding me. I'm so lucky to have her and I've brought her such pain! You said it was crazy to feel this way and maybe I am going a little crazy. When I opened those letters and read that filth, I started to scream at him as if he could hear me. As if I could punish him. And then I ran into the kitchen and smashed everything up. Oh my God, Jake, I should have known! Belle told me about his letters. She made a joke of it, she even called him my little crackpot. But I should have known that Belle never sees danger until it's upon her. She's too strong and self-willed for that. I should have thought! I never even looked at the letters! Now they've long since been thrown away and all we know is his first name. Douglas. Belle has tried and tried to remember his last name but she can't. We called her sister in St. Louis. Belle sent her one of the letters, but she threw it away and can't remember his name either. The only thing we do know is that he works in a record store, but where? The detective keeps telling me they'll track him down, but how, Jake? There are thousands of record stores in Manhattan alone, and who's to say he works in Manhattan?

134

In his letters he said that I knew where to write to him. What is he talking about? I don't even know who he is!

Paul Gross came over last night when I couldn't sleep again. I told him what the letters said as closely as I could remember them. The police have them now. Paul said he sounds paranoid and that sometimes paranoids get side-tracked onto other delusions and never return. But could we ever be sure?!

Oh, Jake, I'm falling apart.

I can't sleep or think of anything but my poor darling Belle.

I will pull myself together. As long as I know Belle is safe, I can make it. Her room is kept locked at the hospital and only authorized personnel are allowed in. The police are sure that he's no longer interested in her now that she's not with me. In his demented mind he was protecting me from her.

No, darling, don't fly in. You have business you must attend to and I'm not alone. David is here and my detective is really more of a psychiatrist anyway. He always knows what to say. His name is Stan Johnston and he has two kids, and God love him, he even knows how to make me smile when I'm not feeling sorry for myself and so wretchedly guilty over Belle. But call me every night, please? Thank you for not thinking less of me because of my constant hysterics.

I will pull myself together.

So much love,

Sal

19th Precinct

Stan—

Lafayette Street has passed the Ross photostats on to Friedman in Washington. He'll get back to you. So far nothing. Nothing on record stores either, according to Burns, but the girls are still trying. Should they start on Brooklyn?

Willy

"Destiny is written in the stars"

May 12th. 12:55 P.M.

Dear Miss Ross:

Lilyan Peters came to see me this morning about you. I am an astrologer and have aided the police in several investigations in the past. In order to be of service, I must first know the exact time, day and date of your birth. Miss Peters told me you are an Aquarian. In general, the next few weeks are ones of peace and contemplation for Aquarians, but I will need more specific information to be of greater help.

Most sincerely yours,
Marna Todd

May 12th, 1976

Dear Sally,

Still no reply from you.

What am I to think? Surely my Sally would not let
so many days go by without a word to her own true love if
there were not a good reason. Surely my Sally would not be
guilty of that kind of callousness. Terrible thoughts have
"crept" into my mind. I am desperately ashamed to admit
them. Doubts about you, my love, my star. But even as
these thoughts assailed me, I knew they had to be groundless. So I set out to disprove once and for all that my
Sally could have any but the most loving and respectful
thoughts of me. I knew that to go too near to your apartment might prove dangerous to us. After all, I do not know
to what extent the police were able to put "two and two
together" after your secretary's little "accident." So I purchased a pair of binoculars (an excellent German set, ridic-
ulously expensive) and went about the business of protecting my love. In the park not far from your residence is a
"grassy knoll" from which one has an unobstructed view of
the front entrance of your building. I was particularly at-
tentive to the doorman with whom your ex-secretary had
her clandestine exchange, but in three days, Sally, at the
moment of mail delivery, that man was only there once!
Other doormen were in evidence on the second and third
days of my scrutiny! Therefore, my letters must have
reached you!

Why then have you not replied to them?

A word, Sally, is all that I ask. No, I do not ask it. I
demand it. In the name of love I demand it. Sally, I have
been so mistreated and maligned by persons I trusted in

the past. It has not been easy for me to place my trust, newly washed clean with hope and love, in you. The torture of doubts has beset my mind. Only you can alleviate these doubts with a sweet tender letter. Do not be afraid to write to me, Sally. Be careful, lest your actions are noticed, but you must now do your part as I have done mine. There must be one trusted person at the theater or at your residence who could mail your letter without being noticed. Think, my darling. One person in whom you trust because of past experiences. A go-between is what is needed at the moment, so that some word of love comes to me to push the painful doubts away and bring me that sweet exquisite joy that only love can cause. I await your letter in much the same state that a drowning man awaits a breath of cool perfumed air.

Despite all these doubts, I worship and adore you.

Douglas

CONTINENTAL STUDIOS

May 12, 1976

Dear Sal:

I'm writing this because every time I start to say it on the phone, you stop me. Let me come to you, Sal. I know you don't need me, but I don't want you to go through this thing alone. If that detective can make you smile, I can make you laugh. I always could.

Now I've said it without interruption.

Love,

Jake

ST. BERNADETTE'S HOSPITAL
678 East 198th St., Bronx, N.Y. 10062

5/12

Dear Bess,

I've got a splitting headache right now, thanks to your call and Sal's visit. I wish to hell you'd both just calm down. He's not after me, he doesn't know where I am, and anyway I'm not a patient in this place any more, I'm a prisoner. If I step foot out of my room, some goddamned nurse moves up alongside me and hustles me back in here. So stop calling me every second. You're driving me nuts. And you're a pleasure compared to Sal. I'm supposed to stay calm so I can get well, but how am I supposed to be calm when Sal keeps crying that it's all her fault? It's nobody's fault, or if it is, it's mine. I was the shmuck who answered his letters. I wish to hell Sal would stop beating herself up over it. Today I wanted to get out of this bed and spank her. I was mad at her the way I used to get mad at Sid for smoking three packs a day. Today she said when this whole thing is over and she can get out of the show, she's taking me on a spree all over Europe. Can you see that? Maybe we'll pick ourselves up a couple of gigolos in Rome and go on a toot. Believe me, I could use one. The one effect this tsurus has had on me is to show me you gotta live while you've got the chance. Enough sitting around worrying over Sid's stone. Maybe I'll let Sal do it. I'd sure as hell like to see Paris. Can you see me with a new face and a flowered dress shlumping up the avenue? I already know how to say yes in French, so I'm halfway there, right?

Now I've heard everything. Sal's detective friend is sending over a guy to talk to me. A hypnotist, if you can believe it. He's going to try to jog my memory so I remember the guy's name. Well, why not? I got nothing else to do with my time except watch television, speaking of which, if you think we got troubles, catch *All My Children* some day. Now that's tsurus. Love to your gang,

                                        Belle

19th Precinct

Stan—

Burns called to tell you nothing in Manhattan and the girls
are half through Brooklyn. Bronx is next. Caplan wants to
know what's happening.

Willy

19th Precinct

Willy,

Tell Caplan what's happening is that yesterday was my eleventh anniversary which I didn't get to go home for and my wife is stinking mad at me and wants me to get the hell out of police work and we're working as fast as we can but nothing's happening, okay?

Stan

Saturday the 13th

Dear Jake,

This morning another letter arrived from him. You know I'm not allowed to open my mail until Stan has seen it. Well, he didn't want me to read it and I didn't fight him. Just seeing the envelope gave me the shudders. But Stan said it was good news and gave them much more to work with. He was almost gleeful. Oh, darling, wouldn't it be wonderful if this was it? I didn't dare ask what the good news was. If it were less than I've hoped for, I don't know what I'd do. I'm so much calmer now I'm almost back to my old self, thanks mostly to Stan and Belle. Stan had a brilliant idea. He's sending a hypnotist over to see Belle, to try to help her remember the man's last name. Belle scoffed at the idea but gave in. That, coupled with whatever was in this morning's letter, may mean we're near the end of this nightmare. Belle continues to get better every day. The way she yells at me, I'm sure she'll be well in no time. I'm going back to rehearsals tomorrow. So you see, the old bag isn't quite the sissy she seemed for the last few days.

I love you like always,

Y.G.S.

P.S. No, don't come. Your place is with Heidi, not me. I'm fine, really. Besides, I only used to laugh because it pleased you.

19th Precinct

Stan—

Why the hell don't you check in from time to time? I'm up to my ass in paperwork and meetings and the least you could do is keep me up on what's happening. Willy tells me you want three plainclothesmen round the clock. Okay, you got them. Is it too much to ask what the fuck for?

Caplan

May 14th, 1976

Dear Sally,

    Oh my darling forgive me my doubts. I am wracked with guilt over having expressed any such base ideas to you. I am a fool is all I can say. But the thought that I may have added to your problems pains me to the core. Of course you are true. You are the truest, most honest, most wonderful person in the world and I do not deserve you. I beg your understanding and your forgiveness. There is nothing I have not nor would not do for you. If I sounded petulant in my letter it is because I yearn for you. I live only for the day when we can put all this behind us and start a life as beautiful and fulfilled as you deserve because of who and what you are and I hope to deserve by my un-failing, unswerving and unquestioning love for you. Do not make me do more penance than I am already "heaping" on myself, I beg you. I await your forgiveness.

                  Yours in body and mind,

                  Douglas

Sally Ross

Dear Lil,

I received your astrologer's letter. Thank you so much, dear, for trying to help, but I really don't put much faith in that sort of thing. As to the exact time of my birth, I haven't a clue. The only thing I remember is my mother saying I set the world's record for labor. I find that difficult to believe, since getting away from that battle ax was always uppermost in my mind.

Belle is strong and sassy again, giving everyone a hard time.

We received another letter from the lunatic, and the police seem to feel it won't be long now. I went back to rehearsals today and I must say, it felt good. Too much sitting around and acting like a weak sister. Belle was absolutely right, I indulge myself too much.

Thanks again for the astrologer, which I won't take you up on, and the offer to come out and stay with you, which I can't. Must stay here so he can write me and make the mistake that puts an end to this whole thing. But I love you for the offer.

Sal

ST. BERNADETTE'S HOSPITAL
678 East 198th St., Bronx, N.Y. 10062

5/15

Dear Jake,

Sal tells me of your concern and well wishes and I feel like a rat for not having written sooner and for not having sent you a congratulation on your wedding. So here it is now. A long happy life to you and yours.

I just had my third session with the swami. Sal told you they got a hypnotist to try to get me to remember the guy's name? Well, you got to see this little number to believe him. He's got a face so full of acne if you connected all the dots you'd probably have a picture of all the major highways across the U.S. If he's so great, why doesn't he talk himself into normal skin? We play this little game together. He tells me to relax. I relax. He says relax some more. I relax some more. He says I'm tense. I say he's full of shit. What a time we have. Between him and the nurses here, I'm really getting ants in my pants to get the hell out of here. Sal has been a doll as always but I'm glad they made her go back to work. Now I can get some rest around here.

So you see, I'm good as new, and don't worry about me. Again, best of luck in the new marriage. I hear she's some kind of knockout. I always knew you had it in you.

Belle

Dear Sally,

Confusion reigns.

Not having heard from you, I knew I had to do something. I was beset with fears for your safety, and so I sat down and made my plans. Logically, coolly, examining all facets to this most perplexing situation. No response from you. Yet, my letters must have arrived. Clearly, then, you are being watched far too closely to permit you to run the risk of communicating with me. I must be more patient. I must be cleverer. I must not give in to petulance or doubt or rash decisions, and I have not, my darling. Your well being is in the hands of someone whose love makes him an "Einstein." I knew that to watch your "comings and goings" from my previous perch atop the grassy knoll in the park might prove a mistake. (If my letters are being intercepted, wouldn't your guards place onlookers there, hovering and lying in ambush, waiting their chance to pounce?) So I took the Fifth Avenue bus at seventy-ninth street. As it moved downtown, past your dwelling, I carefully scrutinized all those on the street, on benches in front of the park, in parked cars. This proved to be no easy task. To be thorough in my examination required no less than six trips. Each time I got off the bus six blocks after your house. I then walked to Madison Avenue and took the bus back to seventy-ninth street, walked to Fifth Avenue and took another bus downtown. And so forth.

It was, to put it mildly, exhausting and expensive. But I did learn the following. One young man in jeans and a jacket that purported to be leather, but even from a distance was obviously vinyl, was seen by me on each and every trip! Standing in the park, sitting on a bench, strolling atop the very grassy area I previously mentioned! My worst suspicions have been confirmed. We are being watched. Do not be afraid, my darling. I will be near, of that you can be sure. But now I must have another round of planning. As in other perplexing situations, he wins who does not move too quickly. Do not misinterpret my stealth as non-caring. It is because I care so very much. Were I to rush in to your dwelling, intent on carrying you away from your persecutors, who knows if my valiance might be to no avail? I am only human and can be overpowered by vile assassins. Therefore, intelligence must rule the day. I shall mail this letter and then sit down carefully and calmly. I pray that you, too, are calm.

My body hardens at the thought of you, my love.

Douglas

May 16th, 1976

Dear Sally,

A second epistle on the self same day!

But necessary, my darling, to tell you what is afoot.
After mailing this afternoon's letter, I went home, made a
cup of strong tea and sat down to think of what could be
done. I am sorry to say that no quick and easy solution
presented itself. Only one need, urgent and overpowering,
gnawed at me—to see you. If only a glimpse from some safe
distance, to assure myself that you are well, to assuage
these yearnings to hold and touch and make magnificent
love to you. (My body cannot control its desires any
longer, my love. I dream of your sweet body every night
and wake to find you gone, but I burn and tighten and
harden from the echos of my dreams and I must relieve myself as best I can. Do not be shocked at this confession. I
would not debase myself if I were free to bring you to the
heights of experience, as I intend one day soon to be permitted.)

So I ventured forth, this time to the vicinity of the
theater, rather than your residence. I was aware that "they"
might be watching both places, but as I say, the need to see
you was utmost. I walked past the theater, careful not to
look directly at it, lest I was being observed. But happy cir-
cumstance! In looking away from the theater, I saw the
small coffee shop across the street, from which I could gain
a perfect vantage point, and so I quickly crossed the street
and went in, taking a seat at the counter from which the
stage entrance was plainly visible. Not knowing how long
my vigil might take, I ordered a large meal, though I was
hardly hungry. A half grapefruit, Salisbury steak, home-

fried potatoes, buttered toast, tea and a sugared doughnut. As luck would have it, I had already purchased a copy of the Daily News, and by pretending to read it, might extend the time even more. Surely the sight of someone lingering over an early dinner, engrossed in the "news of the world" would arouse no suspicion.

Luck was to be on my side today, for hardly had three quarters of an hour gone by when the stage door opened and various persons exited onto the street. From their apparel, I took them to be performers. They all looked tired, so I surmised that the rehearsal was over and that soon my expectations would be satisfied. A lingering look at that most splendid star in the firmament—you! I longed to rush forth at the thought that you might soon be standing mere yards from me, but I knew that would indeed be foolhardy. So I waited.

And then, all my prayers were answered! Wearing a red pullover, apparently of velvet or velour material, black slacks that hugged and revealed your voluptuous body, and a black scarf tied around your hair, you appeared! My heart leapt! And broke. To be so close, my darling, and not to be able to run to you, to hold and caress you! The pain of love, as the poets have said. I know all too well their meaning.

But you were not alone. A man in a grey suit stood with you. He hailed a taxi and you both got in and drove off. Who is he, Sally? I pray he is a mere friend. If not, I will know what to do.

> All the love that the sonnets of
> Shakespeare contain,
>
> Douglas

Sally Ross

Tuesday the 16th.

Dear Jake,

Well, your gal Sal is back again. No more hysterics, no more breast beating, no more acting like a jackass. After rehearsal, Stan and I went to see Belle and had the first real laugh we've had in days. Belle hates her hypnotist, hates the hospital, hates the food, the nurses, her doctor, the view, the lithograph on the wall, everything. God, she was so funny, ranting and raving out of the side of her mouth. She threatened to flash up and down the halls unless they let her out soon. Then she said with what she's got to show, nobody would notice anyway.

It's glorious to be back in harness and, extraordinary as it seems, everybody worked miracles on the show in my absence. (Maybe that's what they needed all along.) It's so much tighter now that they've cut out so much crap and beefed up a couple of parts that needed it. I know I'm supposed to throw a tantrum at the thought of anybody's part but mine being expanded, but Trish is brilliant, and maybe someday she'll be the star and I'll need a favor. The end still isn't there, and I've got a feeling we're going to be previewing until hell freezes over, looking for one.

Last night you asked about David and I hedged. It was too embarrassing to tell you on the phone, darling, and what with my playing the final scene from Camille all over the place lately, I forgot to write you about him. So here goes, if you swear not to throw it up to me later.

David, it turns out, is not precisely almost thirty years old. He is not even—God help me, I can't even write it down—of legal age. David is twenty fucking years old! Twenty. Two-oh. Nineteen plus one. I could die. Jake, how can you tell a man's age these days with all the vitamins they shove in them? In the old days if the beard was dark, they were old enough to vote. Today some of the toddlers I see in the park with their nannies have a two-day growth. And not only is David just this side of puberty, but he still goes to school! (I'm going to be sick, I just know it.) Granted, he goes to school at the Sorbonne, but he goes to school nevertheless. He's a history scholar and had to go back to Paris for the summer session. When he told me, I just sat there, my mouth hanging open, watching this *child* tell me that I had actually had an affair with someone young enough to be my grandson! (It's true. If I were born in the hills of Kentucky and had a child at fifteen and she had a child at fifteen—what am I doing? Someone slap me!) So Thursday I drove my little friend to Kennedy and watched as he toddled onto a 747 for Paris. Then went home and hid under the covers.

I am that portion of a horse that passes through the stable door last.

So now I've told you and now you're having a big laugh. No, not you. You wouldn't laugh at me. You're still my darling Jake who cries at Warner Brother movies and forgives everything. I love you. If you write Belle, don't mention anything about David. I don't want her to know just yet. She'd open her stitches yelling at me. Be well, my darling, and make a million so you can retire to a hilltop with Heidi, have babies and live happily ever after.

Y.G.S.

156

JO COLTON

April 17.

Dear Sal,

Well, Sylvan just returned from town with our tickets. We feel exactly like Madame Ranevsky, yearning to be in Moscow again, not that we've ever been before, but in seven days, we'll be clicking our tourist Brownies like mad in front of the Kremlin. I still feel so disloyal leaving the day before your previews start and with this cloud hanging over you, and we would never do so if you hadn't shrieked like a banshee at me. But in two months when we return all will be perfection. Your show will be a hit, that man will be behind bars in a padded cell where he belongs and we will go for a night on the town that will make history. In the meantime, you have the key to the house. Please, please use it. There's firewood in the basement, tons of food in the freezer and love for you all over the place. Also in the freezer is a small package marked "birds." It's lard. Please put it in the feeder outside the back door and prepare to be awakened at dawn by our greedy neighborhood pets. Will bring you something extravagant and completely decadent from the mother country.

All our love,
Jo and Sylvan

Thursday the 17th.

Dear Jake,

It's almost over, my darling! This morning Belle's sister called from St. Louis. She remembered his name! It's Douglas Green. Stan almost leapt for joy. One more day before previews start. To think, we will have him put away before then!

Oh my Jakila, it's July Fourth, Bastille Day and V-E Day all rolled into one! Love, love, love,

Y.G.S.

Sally Ross

Friday the 18th.

Dear Jake,

This morning two letters arrived from him. Stan read them and said he's sure he's on the verge of showing himself. God, I hope so. Still haven't read the letters, which is just as well.

Incidentally, I was a touch optimistic yesterday. There are 23 D. Greens/Greene's in Manhattan, 20 in Brooklyn, 12 on Staten Island, 19 in the Bronx, 21 in Queens, 14 in Newark and God knows how many on Long Island. When the police computer gets to Philadelphia I'm sure that we'll find the Eastern seaboard is being taken over by D. Greens. And guess what? Not one has had the decency to rush forward and confess. It sure ain't like on Mod Squad. Tomorrow night we have our first Thanksgiving dinner, and I'm the stuffing in the turkey. As Belle would say, I need this?

Y.G.S.

Western Union   Telegram

05/19/76 1253

MS SALLY ROSS, DELIVER BACKSTAGE, DLR

MOROSCO THEATER 217 WEST 45TH ST

NEW YORK NY

JUST REMEMBER WHAT YOU STOLE FROM ME.

LIL

Western Union   Telegram

05/19/76 1207

SALLY ROSS, DLR

MOROSCO THEAT. 217 WEST 45TH ST

NEW YORK NY

IT'S JUST A PREVIEW BUT WE HAD NOTH-
ING BETTER TO DO.

GO BE BRILLIANT. SEE WHAT IT GETS YOU.

DAVID AND GILL

Western Union   Telegram

05/19/76 1251

MISS SALLY ROSS, DLR

MOROSCO THEATER 217 WEST 45TH STREET

NEW YORK NY

TONIGHT I HAD PRUNE JUICE, CREAM OF

MUSHROOM SOUP, PUREED PEAS AND TEA.

ALSO CHOCOLATE ICE CREAM.

SO WHAT ARE YOU DOING?

BELLE

Western Union   Telegram

05/19/76 245P

SALLY ROSS, DLR

BACKSTAGE MOROSCO THEATER 217 WEST 45
ST

NEW YORK NY

SHAKE THOSE FEATHERS, BABY.

JAKE

May 19th, 1976

Dear Sally,

Would that this letter might contain nothing but advice on your first preview of *So I Bit Him*. Would that I could merely ramble on about that unflattering garb in the first act, which is certainly no way to present a star of glamor and allure. Would that all that was on my mind was that tawdry soliloquy that opens the second act, that mundane selection "My Turn" or the choreography which certainly does not show you up to your best advantage. Yes, Sally, I was there. Alas, such advice will have to come later. For now, I am overcome with what I witnessed. No, I do not refer to the show. I refer to the show after the show. But I will relate all that happened in the order in which it occurred.

During the first act I sat gazing up at my own "true love," mesmerized by her genius for theatricality. Although it was evident from the start that the show was far from what it ought to have been. I carefully made my "notes" mentally—which lines worked, which did not, which performers lacked the necessary flair or "presence," which movements seemed extraneous or self-defeating. In other words, all I might draw attention to to aid you in your newest endeavor. It was during the intermission, however, that all "hell broke loose."

I saw that man. You know to whom I refer. The self same man I saw you leave rehearsal with mere days ago. He was standing at the rear of the orchestra, imbibing an orange drink with a woman and another man. I moved closer, disguised as just another member of the crowd. I overheard their conversation—innocuous at best. But then another couple moved into conversation with them and I heard their introductions. The man to whom I have alluded was referred to as "Detective Johnson." Detective! My heart nearly burst through my suit! Surely it was just as I'd imagined. You were clearly being hounded and persecuted by the police! The lights flashed that intermission was drawing to a close, but I could barely find my way back to my seat for the concern I felt for you! When the curtain rose and I saw you I nearly leapt onstage to assuage your fears and to tell you that I was there. How I sat through the second act of the show I'll never know, such was the anguish I felt. But I knew one thing clearly. Somehow, despite the presence of this man, I had to get close enough to give you some sign, some small indication that all was not lost, that I was (as I have always been), at hand and ready to "give my all." So when the final curtain fell, and you finished taking your bows, I walked slowly out of the theater to the stage entrance. A small crowd was already forming, awaiting their chance to see you in person. It was easy to fall in with them, to pretend to be one of those tawdry little people. I waited for what seemed an eternity.

My plan was ingenious. Inside my program I had written a simple message to you. I would merely ask for your autograph, as the others would doubtless do, and as you signed, you would see the message. I knew I could trust you to reveal no sign of recognition, lest we be found out. So I waited, my program carefully opened to that most secretive page.

Others came out of that stage entrance, signed their petty little autographs and melted away into the night. I felt my chest burn for lack of calming air but I waited on. Finally, the door opened and you stepped through, on the arm of that man!

At first I thought he was restraining you but such was not the case. You signed several autographs without his interference. I stepped back in the crowd, too frightened to carry out my task. Then it happened. You smiled at the crowd and started to move off, having had your fill of their presumption. But as you did, you took his arm again. Of your own accord! And I heard you utter the words that made me go cold from head to toe. You said to him, and I am not mistaken, Sally, "You're coming to the party with me and that's that!"

The words stabbed at me like ice cold knives. "You're coming to the party with me and that's that!" Could those be the words of a victim to her persecutor? Of an innocent to her abductor?

And the smile with which you entreated him! I watched as you both hurried off to your party. I stood, riveted to the spot, watching you and this man, this policeman, disappear to your revels.

Sally, what am I to think?

You actually besought the companionship of one to whom we should feel nothing but hatred and loathing! I walked the dark empty streets for hours, tortured with doubts that are best left unsaid. And then it came to me. You are an actress. A consummate actress. Was it mere charade? Were you using your unique God given ability to "pull the wool over his eyes?" I must know. I must know now.

I shall mail this letter immediately and shall expect a reply post haste. It may be dangerous to get in touch with me, but the time has clearly come when we must take the chance. Write the moment you get this letter. Find a

way. After what I have done for you, you must take this
chance for me. As your future husband, I order it.

Douglas

P.S. My message was simply, "I love you. Do not be
afraid."

Sally Ross

Dear Lil,

Thanks so much for the telegram, but I guess I didn't steal quite enough from you. The first preview was a disaster! Besides looking a hundred and ten, I apparently performed that way. Richard Burton was there and gave me one of those terrifying congratulatory speeches in which you say nothing at all. Tell me, Lil, how does retirement work? I'm thinking about going into that line.

Love,

Sal

Dear Sally,

I cannot endure this waiting, this uncertainty, this torture. Sally, the doubts that assail me at every turn! Black horrible thoughts that "worm" their way into my mind!

And still no answer from you!

You must write quickly. Not only to put my mind at ease. There is another consideration. It was meant to be a surprise, but now I see I must tell you.

Sally, I have planned a delightful surprise for you. I know how exhausting preparing a show can be. I know how the endless hours of rehearsal can fatigue one. So I arranged a respite for you. At considerable cost to me, I have reserved a splendid suite at a fashionable resort. It was my plan to take you there Saturday night, after your performance, and to spend the following two days seeing to it that you rest, walk in the sun, eat properly and inhale that revitalizing ocean air.

So you see, you must write to me quickly! Surely, if your smile of friendliness to that detective was a mask of your true feelings, as I pray it was, then that self same charade can be called upon to allow you a moment's privacy to write and post a letter.

Sally, you must do this *immediately*.

Immediately.

If I do not hear from you, what recourse can I have but to think that you have been using me all the while to rid yourself of those you wished gone, with no real concern for me or my well being?

It would be a "bitter pill" indeed if that were the case.

Do not do that to me, Sally. You will never find anyone in this sordid world who can be as good to and for you as I am. That detective you entreated to escort you to your party cannot hope to match my ardor or my physical abilities. I am not overestimating myself when I say I am a lover unlike any you have known. Nature has endowed me in a "grand" way, and all that is mine is yours, if you will but be honest and true to me. I will not write further because it would only delay you in answering me.

Quickly, Sally. Please.

Douglas

19th Precinct

Stan—

Burns' office called. *David* Green of 1231 Ocean Drive, Rockaway, works for a distributor of Motown records.

Willy

Sally Ross

Dear Jake,

Well, the next time you see me if I look like someone's great grandmother, don't be surprised. I just had ten years added to my age from sheer fright.

A few days ago Stan told me not to leave the apartment without him. That didn't sit too well, I can tell you. I promptly went into my now-famous hysterical act. I was sure this meant that the mugger was coming after *me*, but Stan assures me he's not. His letters are still filled with adoration, still pleading with me to write him. God, if only I knew *where* to write him, this nightmare would be over. Stan said it was only a matter of procedures, regulations, etcetera, etcetera. I didn't buy any of it and Stan finally told me the truth. The man has been hanging around, trying to get a look at me. But not, Stan swears, to harm me. Just to look. Okay, so far, so good. I could still have let out a wail that would have awakened the dead, but I'm holding on, right? Right. Little Miss Gutsy. Well, this morning I was sitting around, waiting for Stan to get here and the worst happened. I ran out of cigarettes. I searched under the couch pillows, old purses, pockets, everywhere. Not even enough lint in my pants' cuffs to roll my own. Now, Jake, you know my powers of self-control. I fixated somewhere at the four-year-old level. So, moron that I am, I thought I would take a quick trot around the corner and pick up a pack of True Blues, which are so low in tar and nicotine they're practically good for me. So I disregarded the warnings of Stan and the Surgeon General and left the apartment alone. After all, it was broad daylight, I wasn't going into the subway, the street was full of people, and so forth. I can, if pressed, always supply tons of reasons for acting like a fool, but then you already know that about me. Well, darling, I got what was coming to me. In spades. As I came out of the grocery store, puffing away and thinking how brave I am, I saw him. A young man standing at the corner and pretending not to look at me but staring all the same. You can't fool an actress about something like that. I clutched. Then I remembered that lots of people stare at me. I'm a goddamn celebrity, right? So I puffed my way to the corner and turned west. Jake, he turned, too! Well, you know how short the block between Madison and Fifth is. Not today. By the time I rounded the corner on Fifth, I was practically in tears. So much for your brave little lady. Thank God, the first sight I saw was Stan, just going into the house. I ran to him, shrieking that the man was following me. And then I turned around and there he was! Standing there, pretending he was going to cross the street! Jake, at that moment I felt so many things at the same time I was a one-woman juggling act. Terror, of course. But also joy, because there he was and here was Stan and he could arrest him and the whole horrible thing would be over. Then a moment of Twilight Zone. Stan took me by the arm and led me directly to the man! I don't know how I lived through the twenty seconds it took to get to the corner. Every movie I ever saw was running full speed in my head. Stan was handing me over to the enemy. They were in it together. They were going to kidnap me. I don't know what I thought. But when the sound of my pulse pounding in my ears stopped sufficiently so that I could hear, I found out that the young man who was following me was a plainclothes policeman. It seems I've been watched by the police for days now. Well, talk about your relief, your embarrassment, your almost breaking down and crying on the street like a baby. And then, talk about your lectures! I never saw that side of Stan before. He should give up police work and become a director. But please, Sweet Jesus, not before he catches that man.

So there you have it. Another ordinary day in the life of Sally Ross, who is turning white at the temples and yellow at the back.

Needless to say, I'm giving up smoking. I'm going to eat instead and get so fat that no one, no matter how deranged they are, will ever want my picture again.

All right, I've used your shoulder enough for one day and I'm already hideously late to rehearsal. Stan says he's going to carry me there in his coat pocket. Oh, would that he could!

Love from an ever so slightly shaking ex tobacco addict,

Y.G.S.

P.S. I enjoyed meeting Heidi by phone this morning. She sounded very, very sweet.

May 23rd, 1976

Dear Sally,

Two more days and still no answer. I am at my "wit's end" with you, Sally. I am trying, trying against enormous odds, to withhold any damning judgment of you, but it is not easy. You are, at the very least, irresponsible and uncaring. Yes, and self-centered. At the very worst—no, I will not think that of you. Even in this, my moment of anguish, I do not want to think of you as anything but the Sally I've come to love. True, I now see another side of you, but surely it is not a "black" side. Merely the childlike self-absorbed side of a woman who is used to being treated as if she were the only one who mattered. And generally speaking, that is true. But not in this instance, Sally. In this, I matter, too. If I am to be your life mate, you must treat me with the care and concern with which I treat you. The rest of the world may like or "lump" it, but my feelings must be of utmost importance to you. Otherwise, how are we to have a fulfilled life together? If you've got it in your head that I would be satisfied basking in your shadow, being the kind of man who "fetches and carries," you've got another think coming. Clearly, I have already proven that I am no such spineless jellyfish, and I can prove it again, at any time. But enough, for the moment. I feel myself getting angry with you, and I do not wish to be angry with the woman I love, even if she is not exactly what I would have wished her to be.

The course of true love, the poets have said, does not run smooth. I now understand what they mean. I expect your letter and full apology in the morning. Until then, I will try to think the best of you, but it is not easy when you let me down.

With disappointment,

Douglas

Dear Sally,

After a sleepless night of tossing and turning, of soul-searching and recriminations, I now am forced to send you this, my ultimatum. If I do not hear from you within twenty-four hours, I wash my hands of you. You will have to take care of yourself, since your problems will no longer concern me. There is a limit, even to love. I will not accept this "cavalier" treatment, even from you. You may think that, as a star, it is your due to treat those who care for you with utter lack of concern. But there is more than one kind of star. I am another and as such demand the treatment due me, and not the egomaniacal, heartless way in which you've ignored my letters. One more day, Sally. That is all you have. And if you miss this opportunity, you will never hear from me again. Not all the entreaties, all the vows of love and faithfulness will bring me back.

One day.

Douglas

May 25th, 1976

Dear Sally,

You have lost.

I warned you that I would wait no more than one more day. And yet, you did not answer me.

Very well, it is on your head now. I now believe the unthinkable. You used me for your own ends. You lied and schemed and took advantage of my innocent love for you. You truly are the "bitch" I could not bring myself to believe you were. A self-centered, egomaniacal, ruthless "bitch."

Well, you shall have no more of my attention or my time. You are on your own now, and I'm sorry to say you deserve whatever happens to you. I could not possibly care less. This is what happens when persons who should know better give in to their basest motives. Pipers will be paid and you have run up quite a "bill" with yours.

When I think that tomorrow night was to have been the beginning of our mutual ecstasy, the awakening of our love, the first time we lay down together to drink of each other's bodies.

What a fool I've been.

What a stupid, naive fool.

But even fools wake up, given enough provocation. And you have provoked me, Sally, as no man or woman ever has in the past. You deserve the worst, as that is what you have handed out.

And the worst will undoubtedly come your way, for life has a way of balancing out, as nature has a way of balancing her forms of life. The evil we do is then brought back to our doorstep. You have caused me to do evil on your behalf. It was not evil at the time, for it was done for love. Now I realize I was duped, and my act, my glorious act of love, was contaminated by your viciousness.

I do not know whether to let life catch up with you or whether to take it into my own very capable hands. You must be taught a lesson—of that there can be no doubt. As you doubtless know, I am *very good* at teaching lessons to persons whose nature is arrogant and self-centered. If you don't believe me, ask Belle Goldman. She will tell you something of how I deal with those who would hurt me.

Douglas

May 25, 1976

Dear Sal:

Okay, that's it. I'll be in New York on the 29th, soon as I
tie up some loose ends here. I don't want to hear another
word about it. Baby, who was the one who took care of
me when I had infectious hepatitis? The name was Sal.
Who was it who held my hand when Twentieth fired me?
A kid named Sal. Who made me believe in myself again?
Sal. Who taught me what loving was all about? Sal.

Don't deny me my chance to act the big shot, will you? I
didn't mention on the phone that I'm coming, because
you get so het up with that Irish temper of yours there's no
talking to you. Even Heidi thinks I should go. Besides, a
chance to get away from Franklin doesn't come up every
day.

I was reading my L.A. *Times* this morning over coffee
(You're right, Heidi is sweet. Her coffee, however, is what
they used to give people in prison camps to make them
talk.) and I saw you made the best-dressed list. Very nice,
Miss Flaherty. You've come a long way from Yonkers.

Love

Jake

ST. BERNADETTE'S HOSPITAL
678 East 198th St., Bronx, N.Y. 10062

5/25

Dear Bess,

Well, congratulate me. The shmendrick in white just dropped by to tell me that since I've been such a good girl, they're letting me go home in a couple of days. It's going to be some relief to get out of here. Sal wants me to come stay with her, but to tell you the truth, much as I love her, I'm only comfortable in my own place. I tried to tell her that but it took her detective-in-waiting to convince her it wouldn't be a good idea to have me around the place. I asked him why and he hedged. Got a funny feeling about that. Either something's going on he doesn't want us to know about, or maybe he's just not thrilled with the prospect of seeing a lot of me.

These damn bandages have got to stay on for another month, the shmendrick says. The way the side of my face hurts sometimes, I must be some sight under all the gauze. Quasimodo Goldman, that's me. Tomorrow the plastic surgeon is coming in for a peek. I hope he's got a strong stomach.

To tell you the truth, Bess, I don't feel so hot. But don't get hysterical will you? One of us is enough.

Love to your gang,

Belle

May 26th, 1976

Dear Bitch,

Are you worrying?

I hope so, because believe me, you have a great deal to worry about.

Wouldn't it be too, too dreadful if that adored and renowned face of yours met the same fate as that of your ex-secretary?

Delicious.

Absolutely delicious.

What makes it even more divine is that there's nothing you can do about it. Should you go to the police, you will have to incriminate yourself in the aforementioned assault.

Delicious. Absolutely delicious.

A former friend

Hello again.

A new idea occurred to me and I knew at once that I had to share it with you, my dear, dear Sally. I was browsing through *Hollywood Babylon* this afternoon. You must read it. It's a book that tells about the sordid lives of so many of your ilk and what befell them. All so beautifully justifiable.

Just think! You might be in the new edition!

Ta ta.

A former friend

May 26th, 1976

Dear Sally,

   I heard an absolutely devastating rumor today! It
seems they may increase the cost of stamps!

   Well, then I'd best write you frequently while the
price is still a mere thirteen cents.

   Have you ever considered what it might feel like to
be fucked (pardon my "french") with a meat cleaver?
Now, there's something to contemplate!

                                    A former friend

Dear Sally,

A fourth letter! I do hope you appreciate all the time, creative energy and expense you are putting me through. But then, noblesse oblige. I do owe you these entertainments for all that you have done for me. Sally, a word of warning from a friend. Gossip has it that a certain "gift" has been sent you. My advice is to open all packages *very carefully*, if you know what I mean. I surely wouldn't want anything to happen to you, now would I?

A former friend

19th Precinct

Stan—

Burns called to say they've drawn a blank on D. Greens and all record stores in the metropolitan area. What next?

Willy

Sally Ross

Thursday the 27th

Dear Jake,

Let me try to explain to you calmly and rationally why I
don't want you here. First, your place is with Heidi, not
me. Second, I am not alone. I have policemen constantly
under foot and Belle and all my friends. And rehearsals
and performances and too much to do to put up with you,
my darling.

Now here's the real reason. All my life, Jake, I've manipulated people into taking supporting roles in my life. You
know it's true. If I'd ever let you share top billing in our
marriage we'd still be together. I'm fifty years old now and
my life is not at all what I wanted it to be. And that's
clearly the reason. I know old dogs aren't supposed to
change, but I must, if I'm to get any satisfaction from the
years ahead. So I'm starting now. It's enough that you
want to come. I adore you for it, but I can't fall back into
my old pattern. All it gets you is a big French Rococo penthouse in which you live all alone. Please help me, Jake. I
need, just once in my life, not to be selfish. This is the last
conversation we're going to have about your coming East.

Today Stan and I took Belle out of that awful hospital
and home. She'll have a nurse staying with her, named,
and could I make this up, Miss Priddy Ketchum. Jake,
she's straight out of Dickens. I adored her at first sight but
Belle, well, you know Belle. She had to test her with that
sewer mouth of hers, or rather, half that sewer mouth. But

187

Ketchum hung in there, enjoyed it all, swapped stories about an uncle who was constantly arrested for obscenity and lewdness, and it was only a matter of time before Belle favored her with a few hoo-hoos. You know, I've never been to Belle's house before and what a strange feeling! It was as if I'd never really known her at all. The darling has plastered the place with pictures of me, her husband, who was truly funny looking in a very sexy male way, and her family.

But the biggest surprise of all was that Belle is a painter! The walls were filled with paintings she'd done, and they were really good, Jake! There was one that stunned me. Of a man in the distance on a hill. I think it was probably her husband. There was such love in that painting, such beautiful quiet love! It made me terribly sad to see her paintings and to know that Belle takes the subway down from the Bronx every day to my apartment to type my letters and arrange my day and do work that's so far beneath her. If life were fair, I'd be standing in line at some gallery just to get a glimpse of that man on that hill.

We get a letter from the mugger almost every day now, and Stan says it's the best sign possible. I still refuse to read them (not that I'd be allowed to anyway), but you know me, I never enjoyed looking in the gutter. For every nickel you find, you see a lot of dog shit along the way.

I'm getting a wee bit of a case on Stan, as you may have surmised. And he's still a little awe-struck and shy with me. Terribly cute. He's like a burly, younger you, but without the space between the front teeth. Tell me, is there anything in this world as sexy as a space between front teeth?

Love, love and more love,

Y.G.S.

19th Precinct

Stan, where the hell are you? Can't you stop by my office once in a while? When I put you on the Ross case I didn't think it meant I'd never see your ugly face again. Willy tells me you want two more men. What the hell is that guy, a man or the shadow?

Caplan

May 29, 1976

Dear Sal:

You've never understood that you give as much as you take. I thought that kind of guilt was only for Jews. All right, I won't come. But if you change your mind, for Christ's sake don't keep it to yourself.

Love,

Jake

P.S. If your life isn't what you want it to be, it's because the world is full of idiots. Like me.

Dear Bitch:

I just realized a simply awful faux-pas I unwittingly committed! And I'm so, so regretful. I didn't get you an opening night present.

Now, what to get you? "Hmmm."

They're doing wonderful things these days with guns. Or perhaps poison would be more appropriate. But let me think. What would really be appropriate for such as you?

Fire is such a lovely gift. As I may have mentioned, I've given it in the past and it was so well received. Also knives are always in such good taste.

But messy, don't you think?

I have it! Just the thing. Gorgeous! By the time you receive this letter, you will already have received my "gift." I hope you liked it. There is no one in this world I would rather see have it than you. I do hope it's to your liking, as it is exactly the kind of thing I see you in.

Ciao for now.

A former friend

Sally Ross

Oh, Jake,

It's all so loathsome. So degenerate. I don't know if I can hold out until it's over. But of course you don't know what I'm talking about. I tried to call you but was told you were away for the weekend. I went to the theater yesterday afternoon for the matinee and when I went into my dressing room, oh God, Jake, it's so awful, someone had defecated and urinated all over the place! Not someone. We know who it was. Him. Jake, the police have been lying to me all the time. His letters haven't been filled with love at all. Belle was only his first victim. Now he's after me. Stan tried to deny it, but he couldn't. He says this is exactly what they want—that I'm constantly watched and if he gets near they'll catch him. But why didn't they catch him yesterday in my dressing room?! God, Jake, the police are only men but he seems to be . . . I don't know what he is. It's almost like he's more than a man. Some kind of devil. If only we knew where he was! He still thinks I do. Oh, Jake, I'm frightened. I'm truly, truly frightened. If only I believed in God. You do. Make me believe in God, too, Jake. Otherwise, how am I going to get through this?

Sal

19th Precinct

Willy, Arrange twenty-four hour surveillance on the Morosco. Get Bridges up to the Goldman house in the Bronx. Find out where Stan is and have him call me.

Caplan

May 30th, 1976

Dear Bitch:

Well, was it everything you had hoped for? The colors, brown and yellow, are you! I only wish I had been able to give you your gifts in person. To "shower" them on you, as it were. Instead of just "plopping" them down and running, but you know what a heavy schedule I'm on these days. So much to do. So very many social obligations. It's all too too tiring. But fear not, Sally, I can always find time for you. And I do have another gift in mind. Of a more lasting nature. The kind of gift one only gets once in a lifetime, because one can only use it once in a lifetime. Can you guess what it is, you clever, clever bitch? That's right. I am going to kill you.

Now, how shall we arrange it? You don't take the subway, and you have that cute little policeman with you.

"Hmmmm."

I will find a way. You know I will. There's nothing you can do to stop me.

By now you must have surmised that I am no ordinary person and so it will be in no ordinary way.

It's all too divine, my darling.

A former friend

May 30th, 1976

Dear Phil,

Best to you and Ginnie, and am still smarting for not having seen you two way back when. Next trip we'll definitely get together and set the town on its ear.

Phil, I've got a little problem. Sally's going to do a TV special in a few weeks, where she plays an assortment of roles. You know the type show. Sketches, songs, dances, as only my Sally can do them. The problem is this. In one of the sequences she portrays a German spy in the Second World War, for which she needs the use of a Luger pistol. Well, believe it or not, we are having one hell of a time finding one. Also, there seems to be this law that if a performer uses a gun on a show, you have to have two policemen on the set. Can you believe it? Our producer, madman that he is, refuses to open the set to anyone, not even the police! The whole thing is one swift pain in the ass, let me tell you. But this morning I remembered that you used to have a Luger from the days when you were into collecting Nazi mementos. So, the favor is, have you still got it, is it in working condition (she's supposed to fire a few blanks) and can we borrow it for a week or so? It would really make things easier, and I'd sure as hell appreciate it. Tell you what. You loan us the gun and next time you and Ginnie come to town, Sally and I will make sure you have a time to tell your grandchildren about, okay?

Your friend,

Douglas Breen
780 West 71st Street
New York City

May 30, 1976

Dear Belinda,

Couldn't reach you but wanted you to know that Quentin and I are going out to East Hampton for the next few weeks. It's all because of that Ross woman next door. Evidently, there has been some kind of a threat on her life. That's what the building talk is. But the point is you can't go out or come in without being stopped by guards and the place is overrun with them. Even the delivery boys are checked in and out. Last night, Quentin's junior partner was stopped and searched on his way in! I can't tolerate it any more and so we're off to the peace of the shore. I can't tell you what it's like to live next door to that woman. If it's not one thing it's another. Will call you in a few days.

Fondly,

Edith

Dear Bitch:

Well, it's all been too too tiring. What has? Why, deciding how to kill you, my dear. I want you to know all I'm going through for you so that you truly appreciate my efforts. Today I dashed out and did some comparison shopping on your behalf. Have you any idea of the price of a rifle with telescopic lens? My dear, they must think they're selling pure gold! But then everything is so high these days, isn't it? I saw a darling pistol, however, which was within my price range. Then I got to thinking, I'd have to get awfully close for it to do any serious damage to you, and there's still that policeman to deal with.

A word of warning. If you're thinking of telling the police where to find me and pretending you had nothing to do with your secretary's "accident," may I remind you of a few things. I would not hesitate for a moment to let the world know that the whole thing was your idea. I was merely your tool. I understand that before one loses consciousness in the gas chamber the odor of cyanide causes one to choke to death on one's own vomit. And frequently, one jolt of electricity in the electric chair is not enough to kill, merely to cause agony.

At least, I will be merciful.

Then, too, I might change my mind, mightn't I?

But then again, I might not.

What a quandary!

A former friend

Sally Ross

Dear Jake,

Forgive me for hanging up on you, but you mustn't come. If you were here and anything happened to you, I couldn't bear it. The police have their hands full watching me. They can't watch both of us. And I don't want you to see me the way I am. I'm not doing well, Jake. Please just let me go through this without the added shame of your seeing me.

Don't worry, my darling. I'm never alone now. Besides Stan, there's a policewoman who sleeps here every night. So you see, he can't get to me. Why doesn't that knowledge make it easier for me? I walk through the show and race back home—the only relaxation I get is during my visits to Belle. She's so strong and I'm so weak.

But I will change, if it isn't too late.

Oh, Jake, pray for me, will you? I'd do it myself but I'm not that much of a hypocrite.

Sal

198

Dear Sally,

I have just had one of the most delightful afternoons, thanks to you, and I simply had to sit down and write my favorite bitch all about it.

It all started last night when I went to dinner at a local eatery, The Golden Spoon. The food is, at best, undistinguished, but the ambiance is pleasant enough and the prices not unduly high. As I was sitting there dining on a somewhat overdone cheeseburger and soggy French fries, my gaze happened to wander to two "gay" boys sitting nearby. Why these degenerates are called "gay" is obvious. They chattered away like deluded magpies, their voices shrill and all too animated. Of course, their hands moved in unison with their speech, so that they had the appearance of fluttering Southern "belles." (Belles? Belle Goldman? Is there a connection here? Freud has said there are no accidents, you know.) At any rate, not to digress further, it occurred to me that these denizens of the third world were more like girls than boys. Indeed, one of them had the habit of "tweezing" his eyebrows in the style of women.

What a sight these perverts were! And what a splendid idea they gave me!

The next morning, awash with enthusiasm, I sallied forth to my appointed rounds. (Another! Sallied forth. Sally. Is it any wonder that Sigmund Freud occupies a place of honor in history?) First, to a women's clothing store where I purchased a loose blouse of Indian fabric, a brassiere (Oh, the amusement of explaining to the shopgirl that my "wife" was as wide across the chest as I am.) Then on to a shoe store to purchase a pair of women's flat-heeled shoes. (Again, explaining to the girl that my "wife's" feet were the same size as mine! I don't think she believed me. Perhaps she thought me to be one of "them" desirous of purchasing shoes for myself!) All so droll. My last stop was the Five and Ten to purchase an inexpensive woman's wig and a few articles of make-up. Then home with all my purchases to start the transformation. Yes, Sally, by now you must have guessed my intent, being the clever little bitch you are.

But what a job!

I started with my own jeans, since jeans are, these days, unisex. I donned them and studied myself in the mirror. An obvious problem. At the risk of being risqué, I must make mention of my male organ. As I have mentioned, I am opulently endowed. Almost ten inches when erect. This is not self-aggrandizement. Such has been proven with the aid of a ruler. Now see what your cruel behavior has denied you!

I might add, not only is my "organ" of that superior length, but in width I am also a very very extraordinary man. Suffer, my darling. It will never be yours. But I hereby give you permission to dream of it if you like. And to imagine it towering over you, at full extension and reddened with lust. Dream on. You have thrown out that "baby" with the bath water, as they say. But back to my dilemma. How to disguise the bulge that my manliness caused in those jeans. (A bulge that had been much admired by "gay" boys as they have passed me in the street, I might add. But let them stare and suffer, too.) I took off my jeans and put on a tight swimsuit beneath them. Though uncomfortable, to be sure, it did hide my endowments. Then, with great difficulty, I put on the afore-mentioned brassiere and stuffed the cups with tissue paper. My appearance was, at this point, most amusing. Half virile man, half not terribly attractive woman. I donned the wig. Better. The blouse. Still better. Then came the most difficult chore. To transform my face into that of a woman. To start, I inserted a new blade into my razor and shaved closely—a bit too closely, for my face became reddened in several areas. But the face powder I had purchased hid those telltale blotches. Then to the lipstick, applied lightly and with finesse. Nothing gaudy, nothing cheap. Just a light veneer of "Blushing Pink" as it was named. On to the eyes. Oh, I do not understand how women can apply liner or coloring to their eyes! One surely needs another set of eyes to oversee the application! I was most amused by the whole procedure, which took three tries before it passed my standards. I then beheld myself in the mirror, only to find that I had neglected to change shoes! Having done this last chore, I examined myself again. Surely I would offer no threat to the beauties of the street, but I did have the appearance of a somewhat ordinary young woman. The effect was excellent, but somehow, slightly unconvincing. I practiced the walk of a woman. Not the mincing strut of a transvestite or the brazen waddle of a queer, but the normal unselfconscious walk of a true woman. I must hand it to myself—I was superb. Still a doubt haunted me. If there were only a final touch, some completely feminine attribute I might add to my already transformed self. And then it came to me! A stroke of ab-solute genius! What is the one physical endowment only a woman can possess? A pregnant stomach! Delighted with my new idea, I took a small needlepoint pillow from my couch, a gift from a certain young woman who at one time thought she might trade various presents for the use of that gloriously aforementioned male "organ." I taped it round my stomach under the blouse and studied the effect.

Perfection!

And an added bonus. By appearing pregnant, any discrepancy in my "walk" would be instantly dismissed by onlookers!

Do I hear applause from you, Sally? Surely, by this time, I deserve it.

Then, to my deed.

Once again, I found myself on the corner of seventy-ninth street and Fifth Avenue, waiting for the bus. I got on with no unusual looks from anyone. I was completely accepted on my appearance.

And then, the coup!

I got off the bus just across the street from your residence, strolled to the corner, crossed the street and walked casually as you please right past your building! The doorman did not even glance my way! What sheer delight and power. I then came home and transformed myself back to my own blessedly male state. No, Sally, it was not my intention to seek admittance in that garb to your building and apartment or to accost you in any way. It was a mere charade, a cat and mouse game, meant only to show you how you are at my mercy.

When and if I kill you, Sally, it will be as myself, not in the disguise of anyone else. For surely this is a pleasure that only I of all persons am entitled to.

You have, in the past, brought me joy. Now you bring me titillation. (Another of those wondrous double entendres?)

Soon you will bring me ecstasy of a sort I never dreamed of.

An ecstasy fuller and richer than even the act of love itself.

The ecstasy of death.

A former friend

June 2, 76

Dear Doug,

Sorry but when Ginnie and I got married my mother
went on a rampage and cleaned out my room. Not only did
she throw away all my Nazi collection, but what's even
worse, my whole collection of EC comics, which would
have been worth a fortune! Wish I could have helped
you out. I don't understand why it's so hard to find a
Luger in New York of all places. Have they tried adver-
tising in Buy-Lines? Good luck with the show. You really
are getting to be a big shot, aren't you?

Phil

Wednesday the 2nd.

Dear Jake,

Thank you, darling. I know what I'm putting you through with my constant calls, but the sound of your voice is the only thing that helps. That and the pills Paul gave me, and I suppose I'm overusing both. Paul said to take one if I was calm, two if I wasn't. I've taken four already this evening.

Jake, I think about us so much of the time now, about what we had together and what we didn't. There's so much to regret. Sometimes it seems life is more regretting than living.

I want so badly to make up to you for all the rotten things I did. Oh, darling, you deserved so much better than me.

I want to confess something to you, Jake. Something I couldn't bring myself to say on the phone because you were so caring and supportive and I was so ashamed. I've held something over you all these years, Jake. I've made you feel guilty and I had no right to. I always knew about you and that girl from Paramount. I knew when it began, when you and she would meet for lunch, and when you started spending evenings with her. I knew you were with her on that weekend in San Francisco. Do you remember what I did when you returned from that weekend? Remember the presents and how sweet and caring I was? It wasn't because I was afraid of losing you. I knew you loved me and not her. It was to hurt you, Jake. To take advantage of your goodness and to make you agonize with guilt so that you'd never never do that to me again. The night you returned, when you thought I was asleep, I lay there and listened to you cry and I was glad. I heard the man I loved sob like a baby and I reveled in it.

Forgive me, Jake. I know why you needed her. Because of me. Because I had robbed you of your dignity, your manhood and your self-esteem.

You turned to her not to get away from me but to be able to stay with me. And I knew it. Don't hate me for knowing it, Jake. If I could, I would have told you and either been understanding or screamed like an outraged wife. Something fair. But the only fair thing I ever did was to let you go. I was fair in that, wasn't I? I'm a kind of vulture, Jake, and the worst of it is that I don't mean to be. As far back as I can remember I've had a kind of raw hunger in me—hunger that goes so deep I've forgotten what it is. But it makes me do things that are cruel and stupid. It made me treat the only man I've ever loved badly.

Oh, Jake, you were right to go to San Francisco! The wonder is that you never went again. You should have. You should have done anything you needed to do to fight me. To get out of life what I refused to give you. I loved you so much, Jake, but the hunger was too great. Now you have a new life—one that will give you everything I was too crippled to give, and I'm so happy for you.

I wish you a child, Jake. I wish you a son. I wish you peaceful nights and laughter and everything we should have had.

God, these damned pills are really something. I can barely read what I'm writing. If it's coming out upside down and backwards I'm sorry, but I've got to wipe our slate clean so that you can remember me with love, just in case. No, I'm not being hysterical about the mugger. I now know what he plans to do. You see, today when Stan was out of the room, I did a stupid thing. I took one of the letters from his jacket and read it. He's going to kill me. And I really don't think anybody can stop him. The funny thing is, I don't know how I feel about it anymore. I've been afraid for so long, I'm getting numbed to it. When I look back on my life, I think I've done everything I'm capable of doing. If that's true, is life so dear that I should fight for it or would it be better to let it go, like I let you go? I could have kept you, Jake. I could have used your guilt and kept you. I suppose the fact that I didn't is something in my favor.

I wish I could sleep. I wish I could walk out on the show. I wish either he'd kill me or they'd kill him. If this is ever over and I'm still alive, I'm going to do something. I don't know what it will be, but I know I've got to do something to make the years that are left better. Who knows, perhaps I could get back to that hunger and finally find out what it is. Even that would be something. To understand why Sally Flaherty needed everything and ended up with nothing. I'm sorry, darling. I'm being self-pitying and ugly. It's the pills.

Have a child, Jake. Please.

I love you.

                                                          Sal

19th Precinct

Stan—

Burns has the girls checking every Green and Greene within a ten block radius of The Golden Spoon. He's also put some of them in the streets to check mailboxes in case there are any shared apartments with a Green among them.

Willy

Dear Detective Johnson;

Although we've never met, I hope you'll pardon my presumption in writing to you, care of Sally. You see, I am that individual you have been searching for. The man who had that little "set to" with Belle Goldman, a fact for which I now feel more than a little regret. There are, however, so many mitigating circumstances of which you know nothing. Things are frequently not what they seem to a casual outsider, I assure you. And the full facts, were they to be revealed to you, would surely make your hair stand on end, as it were.

That brings me to the reason for this note. I am now willing to reveal to you and you alone the full facts, subtle innuendos and hidden meanings behind the aforementioned "set to."

I will not, of course, set them down in this letter, lest "certain well known personages" are precognizant of what I have to say and thereby given the time to plot their "alibis."

No, these facts will have to be given person to person.

Now, I am not such a fool that I would tell you where to meet me. That would indeed be foolhardy! For who knows if you would do the honorable thing or the dishonorable, by which I mean arriving with others and the intent to incarcerate me for my actions. I assure you, once you know the "whys" and "wherefores" of my actions, you would have no such intent. I am far from the villain in this case. I am the victim, and it is as such that I come to you.

I wish to end this "cloud" which hangs over me. I wish exoneration. I wish to continue on the path of my life with my "escutcheon" untarnished.

Therefore, I make the following request. On the corner of Eighth Avenue and Forty-Eighth Street is a public telephone booth, the number of which I jotted down this morning. It is on the northwest corner and stands solitary on that most sordid of streets. (To veer from the subject for a moment, as a police officer, can you possibly excuse the lack of action in cleaning up that neighborhood? The denizens of those streets surely would be better off in a controlled community which caters to their nefarious needs. Somewhere in the mid-west, perhaps. I am not speaking of a prison, for I know that our court system at present is deluged with such cases, and the necessity of trial by jury for each and every one of these specimens would make any action in the next decade improbable if not impossible. What I am suggesting, however, is a community wherein such unsavory characters might be detained awaiting final judgments and verdicts as to their guilt. In this way, the criminal element which now is free to run amok in our streets would be removed, and decent citizens and children would be freed to amble calmly and without fear in their own community. Think it over. It would also have the added benefit of giving jobs to many unemployed persons. Guards, cooks, social workers, etc. Was not such a project undertaken during the Second World War for our resident Japanese?)

But now, back to my request. As I said, I have jotted down the number of said phone booth. My suggestion is that you appear there at three o'clock next Tuesday afternoon and take possession of the booth, so that no one else could unwittingly stand in the way of our conversation. I will call you at precisely three-twenty. (Allowing you twenty minutes to have the booth to yourself, should there be someone calling at your time of arrival.) I will then call you and tell you all that you wish to know—all those hidden aspects of which you know nothing.

Now, a word of advice, to save you some difficulty. I have no doubt that upon receiving this letter, you will immediately contact the telephone company and have any and all calls to that booth traced. I am no fool, nor do I rely on the discretion of people I do not personally know. I do not mean to be offensive. You may indeed be the most honorable of gentlemen, but as of the moment, I have no indication of same. Therefore, I shall call you several times for short durations from several public pay phones I have already "staked out." The calls will last at most one minute each and will require a respite of five minutes or so between them so that I may reach my next pay phone. I would assume the entire transaction to take the better part of an hour, so please plan to have that time free for our conversation. If uninterrupted, I can give you the full facts so that you can then decide what is to be done. I am quite sure that after our conversation, you will see there is no need to bother yourself further with Sally Ross or the entire Belle Goldman case, thereby freeing you to do more important and needed work. What with the police cutbacks that plague our city, I am sure that would please not only you, but also your police commissioner.

Until next Tuesday at three, I remain, yours truly,

The Man You Have Been Searching For

June 4th, 1976

Dear Phil,

Don't worry about it. As it turns out, Sally's crazed producer decided to have the German sketch rewritten and updated to America in the fifties. I got a gun two days ago. Sorry about the comics, though.

Your friend,

Douglas Breen
780 West 71st Street
New York City

CONTINENTAL STUDIOS

June 5, 1976

Dear Sal:

I want you to know everything about that girl and me so
that you'll know I was the one to blame and not you.
Never you, Sal.

I didn't have an affair with her. I just let you think so.
You had just agreed to do another picture and leave me
for two months. That's why I did it. To make you stay.

You were always the straight one, Sal. It kills me to see
you torture yourself. Our marriage went bad for only one
reason. I wasn't good enough for you. But I did love you,
Sal, and I still do. That'll never change. Please forgive me
if you can.

Jake

213

BELLE GOLDMAN

Dear Bess,

Well, the shmendrick says I'm coming along fine, but he doesn't want me to go under the knife before the fall. They're going to fix me up with some kind of partial face mask for the summer. What a life. Did I write you I got a cop here during the days now? It's getting to be quite a bingo parlor. Me, Ketchum, my cop, Sal, her cop, what a group. But at least now there's a real chance it may be over soon. The nut's going to talk to Sal's cop on the telephone tomorrow. Probably to repeat all that crap about Sal helping to plan his attack on me. Jesus, this guy's so nutty he even gives crazy a bad name. What the hell is he thinking with? What does he think all these cops are doing around here if they believe that bullshit? Well, for once I'm glad he's as nutty as he is because maybe he'll buy what the cops are planning to do. They're going to try to convince him that they believe it and that if he testifies against Sal, they'll let him off. Anything, just to get to that bastard. I hope Sal's cop is a good talker.

Meanwhile, Sal is in terrible shape. I don't understand what's happening to her. I know this is no picnic, but she's folding up like I never saw her before. My poor baby, she's taking so many goddamn pills. I told her to lay off the stuff but she says she can't sleep. Also, she refuses to postpone that stinking show, even though the producer said he was willing. She keeps talking crap about always letting people down and that's why all this is happening. She won't lay off the pills, she won't see a shrink, she won't listen to reason. She looks like hell. I just don't understand it but it's breaking my heart.

I don't know, maybe Sid is better off where he is than the rest of us are here. You know what the worst of it is? Sal reminds me of Sid's last months, when he knew he was dying and there was nothing anybody could do. The way he went into that terrible calm where I couldn't make him laugh or smile or even get mad at me. It's happening to Sal now, but Jesus, it's not the same thing! They'll catch that bastard. Why does she have to do this to herself? I swear on Sid's memory, the minute this is over, she's going to a shrink if I have to put a gun to her head. I mean it. I'm not going to stand by and watch her go the way Sid went, without a fight.

All right, so now I'm upset enough for one day. I'll sign off and play pish-pasha with Ketchum. I taught her the other day. She stinks but at least it keeps her shut up for a while. Otherwise, by now I'd know the unabridged story of her whole meshuganah family. Love to your gang,

Belle

19th Precinct

Rivera—

Caplan wants you to cover for Stan at the Ross penthouse
for the next few days. 941 Fifth. Stan should be back to
relieve you in a couple of days. His leg is stiff but it was
just a flesh wound.

Willy

Sally Ross

Dear Jake,

Everyone close to me is in peril. First Belle, now Stan. How could he shoot him in that telephone booth and still get away? He's not human, Jake. He couldn't be. I'm not allowed to leave the apartment now to see Belle or to go to rehearsals. But it won't make any difference. I'm going to die. I know it. I remember when my mother died I felt nothing. No grief. That's the way it'll be for me, too. She had morphine up to the end, and I have my pills. I did bring you some happiness in all those years, didn't I? I never brought my mother happiness. I hated her. It's a terrible sin to hate your own mother. I wished her dead. And now someone wishes me dead. That's not so unfair, is it, Jake? God, I wish I could see you once more. They won't let you come. Don't try.

I did bring you happiness. Don't let Belle stay alone in New York. Make her move to California and don't mind her complaining. It's just the way she is. She doesn't mean anything by it.

I want to sleep. I'll write you every day until it's over.

Sal

P.S. There's nothing to forgive. It wasn't your fault, darling. It was mine.

Dear Sally,

I see in today's paper that Gretchen Wyler is playing your role in previews of *So I Bit Him*. Whyever? Are
you too frightened to pursue your own all-important career? Or have I finally demonstrated to you that there are
things in this world even more important than your blessed
stardom?

I'm sorry to have killed your little detective, but he
left me no choice. He was always with you, you see, and I
had to show you that nothing can stop me. Why are they
keeping it out of the papers? I suppose they have their
reasons, but it does seem peculiar. Isn't the public entitled
to know everything about their sacred cow, you?

I truly am sorry to have killed him. He might have
been a good person. But it has made my mind up on one
thing. I will harm no one else. Except you, my darling. I
will of course kill you.

It was so simple. I merely hid on a low rooftop and
awaited him. Simple, simple, simple.

It will of course be just as simple to kill you.

Last night I dreamt of us, as it was in the old days.
We dwelt in a mansion of many rooms, sun and flower
filled, bursting with joy. You gave yourself to me several
times in that dream and the ecstasy surpassed my wildest
desires. (I did "soil" my bedding during the dream. I took
this to mean neither salaciousness nor lust, but merely that
the deepest kind of love can reach from beyond the con-

scious mind to the "real" world around us.) In the dream you told me you forgave my every action and that you understood they were necessitated by my love for you. You were so understanding, loving and wise. But of course, that personage was only my vision of you. The truth is so much more sordid.

You must return to the show. Gretchen is marvelous, of course, but can you deny the world that special magic that is yours alone? Can you be that selfish? Of course you can. I forget to whom I am speaking. Soon, Sally. I shall kill you soon. I tire of this charade and yearn to go on to the rest of my life, unfettered by my relationship with you.

I have decided to be merciful. You will not suffer, that I swear.

You see, strange as it seems, I do still regard you with vestiges of love, although I know you to be the kind of woman no one should love. Surely you did not choose to be what you are and for that reason I will have compassion.

Soon, Sally. Soon.

Douglas

Sally Ross

Dear Jake,

    I have a nurse now. Paul thought it best. I don't know what's happening to me. The pills, I suppose. She only gives me one at a time but they don't work. When I finally drift off to sleep, it's worse than when I can't. When my mother died she used to stare out of the hospital window, hour after hour, as I stare out of my window now. The city is so beautiful. Do you remember how beautiful it was in the forties? I was beautiful, then, too, wasn't I? And you, so sweet and shy and strong. Think of all the people who died before they were old enough to know how beautiful life is. One pill at a time and no liquor. She makes me tea. Can you imagine that? It's funny, isn't it? I'm not frightened any more. It's a blessing not to be frightened. I've always been frightened, did you know that? When I was little, sometimes the fear was so great I'd hide for hours. But I'm not frightened now.

Sal

June 10th, 1976

Dear Sally,

Another dream of you as you once were. We were walking, hand in hand, and you stroked my face and told me you loved me. And the light that shone from your eyes! I can't bear what has happened to us! I can't bear hating the only person I've ever loved! Is it possible I've misjudged you? Is it possible you wanted to write and come to me but knew that would lead my enemies to me? I am plagued with doubts. If that were the case, then I would be guilty of horrendous crimes against you. If only I could see you, speak with you, hear the utterances I yearn to hear from your own lips. I want so much for you to be what you were to me. I want us to have that which we had in the past. If I have been wrong, what can I do? How would you ever forgive me? I would forgive you anything, Sally, if only I knew I was mistaken. I want, more than life itself, to love you again.

Douglas

CONTINENTAL STUDIOS

June 11, 1976

Dear Sal:

I've never been any good at putting words together to express how I really feel, but now I've got to try. I'm afraid for you, honey. Not only because of that man, but because of something in you. Something that was always there but is exploding out of all proportion and threatens you as much as he does.

In one of your letters you wrote about the hunger in you. I know it. I saw it all the years we were together. I saw something else, too. A way you have of hiding, of covering up what you really feel. It's as if you think the real Sally Flaherty needs to be hidden away for fear that if people saw her they'd run. It's why you always checked yourself from the outside. Why you cared so much what people thought about David. And probably why you became Sally Ross in the first place. Sal, I swear to you there's nothing in you that needs to be hidden away. You don't deserve any punishment, honey. You've never done anything to earn it. I wish to God I could help you, but I don't know what to do. Please, Sal, please go easier on yourself. When this thing is over, we'll tackle that voice that's in you, telling you all those lies about yourself. I agree with Belle. You ought to see an analyst, but not out of guilt or shame. Out

of a simple need to be better to yourself than you are.
Please don't take so many pills and don't drink. It's making it all worse. I love you.

Jake

224

Sally Ross

Friday

Dear Jake,

No sleep again. I wandered through the apartment in the middle of the night and by accident woke up the policewoman who stays with me. She came charging out of her room with a gun. With a gun, Jake! It's all so funny.

I'm not going to stay here any more. I don't care what happens. I can't stay in the apartment any more. I'm going to go away. I know they won't let me, so I'll have to leave at night when she's asleep. I know where I want to be and what I want to see before I die. I'll leave tonight. I didn't tell you when I spoke to you because I knew you'd try to stop me.

I love you. Goodbye.

Sal

Dear Sally,

What can I do? After what I did to that detective, I know they won't permit you to leave your apartment to talk to me. I can't get your number, for it's unlisted. I must talk to you. Please, please, Sally, call me. You know my address. I can't give you my phone number, lest they read this letter, but you can look it up. Please call me, Sally. Guilt hounds me at every turn. Despite everything I've done and said, I love you. You know I do. Please steal away from them and come to me. I won't harm you. I never would have. Do not be afraid. I will not implicate you in either attack. The fact that you have not told the police where to find me leads me to think you do care for me, for surely it can not be only fear that keeps you silent. I must be wrong. I'd die for you, Sally. If you don't forgive me, I will die for you.

Douglas

Sally Ross

Dear Jake,

She caught me last night. But not tonight. I have three pills I didn't take. I'll crush them and put them in her dinner. I only hope he doesn't kill me before I get there.

You always made me so happy.

Sal

June 12th, 1976

Dear Sally,

It's hopeless, isn't it? I have murdered more than a man. I have murdered our life together and the only love I have ever known.

I know now that there is no way out for us. Life without you is meaningless. You were not to blame for anything, Sally. I attacked Belle Goldman without your knowledge. Show this to the police. You had nothing to do with it. I alone did the deed. You are completely innocent. I swear this and want this letter taken down in testimony should you be accused of any wrongdoing. You are innocent. I alone am to blame, and I mean to save the world any expense at my hands, for I have been my own judge and jury and I find myself guilty. Guilty of assault. Guilty of murder. But most of all, guilty of abusing and torturing the only person in this world who ever cared for me.

I will do what is right.

For you, Sally.

I have never loved anyone but you and I will love you until the moment I die.

I wish you a life filled with joy, for that, and that alone, is what you deserve. You are a God to me.

Douglas

19th Precinct

To Braddley, Riegan and Brent—

Be in Caplan's office at three. Sally Ross disappeared last night and you're to work with Stan Johnston on the case.

Willy

Western Union   Telegram

06/12/76 1384

MR. JAKE BURMAN, DLR

CONTINENTAL STUDIOS

LOS ANGELES, CAL.

SAL HAS DISAPPEARED. DO YOU KNOW WHERE
SHE IS? COULDN'T REACH YOU. I'M SICK WITH
WORRY. DID SHE COME TO YOU?

PLEASE CALL QUICKLY.

BELLE

JO COLTON

Sunday

Dear Jake,

It's done, and now I'm alone—finally, mercifully alone. And so peaceful, my darling.

I walked up and down beside the ocean this afternoon. It's so utterly beautiful. The waves, Jake! How wonderful they are! The same waves that have been washing up since before men existed. That's why I wanted to be here. To see the ocean and the sky. Just to have seen it, to have experienced the incredible grandeur of the world even for a brief moment is enough. Could there be anything more beautiful?

I've come to understand so many things in the past few weeks. It's as though I've come through a long dark passageway into the blessed light. It really doesn't matter what happens now. If he kills me or if he doesn't. Because I've seen the ocean and the sky. There were sandpipers on the beach. Their lives are so short and yet still glorious. You see, it really doesn't matter how long life lasts. The point is just to glimpse it, if only for a moment.

I love you. I've always loved you. I always will love you. You, Belle, the ocean and the sky. What a rich life I've had!

And if it's over, well then, it's over. If he kills me today, know that my last thoughts were of you.

Sal

June 15th, 1976

Dear Sally,

By the time you read this letter I will be dead. I die willingly for the torment I have caused you. I die happily because my death proves that I loved you as few men have ever loved before me. I die joyously for I have known the joy of your love. I thank you for that love. I beg your forgiveness for all that I have done to pain you.

And if, as the poets and sages have said, there is a life after this, I will "but love thee better." And we will be together again.

Goodbye, my Sally, my dearest, my love.

Douglas

19th Precinct

Stan—

I sent the photographs of the charred body of the Ross assailant to Harris downtown, as well as photostats of the letter to her that was with the body. Caplan says now that the Ross case is wrapped up he wants you back on Williams. Anderson is getting nowhere.

Willy

BELLE GOLDMAN

6/18

Dear Bess,

I'm sitting here in Sal's apartment having my second gin and tonic (all right, my third), Sal's in the tub singing with the radio and I'm so happy I could bust. I intend to get so roaring drunk that her majesty next door will move to Connecticut. Up yours, penthouse C!

Look, I deserve it. I've had a couple of days that would put a Mack truck in its grave. Until Jake finally called to tell us where Sal was, I thought I'd drop dead from fear. I thought he had her. Then when we found out he killed himself, oh, Bess, I never in my life knew what relief was until that moment. It was as if Sid came down himself to tell me everything was okay. But what a way to kill yourself. Jesus H. Christ. He poured gasoline all over himself like one of those crazy monks. And the letter he left Sal! All I can say is thank God it's over.

My poor Sal. What she's been through! When we got to Shelter Island, she was sitting there in the house, staring out at the ocean, just waiting. For him, I guess. When we told her he was dead she just looked at us. First at Stan, then at me, back and forth. For a minute I got scared that she really had flipped out, but then, thank God, she started to cry. Softly at first, like a baby, Bess. Like a newborn. All the way back to the city I held her in my arms and she cried like that. To tell you the truth, so did I. Yeah, the two old bags sat in the back seat crying like babies, and Stan sat up front beaming like a moron. I like that one.

He's my date for opening night, you know. Don't get excited—he's married. Tomorrow Sal goes back into rehearsals. They say the show's in pretty good shape now and she ought to be able to take over in a week. So opening's been set for week after next. She'll do it. Whatever happened to her, it's over now and she's coming around. She slept for twenty-four hours straight. No pills. No booze. I watched her sleeping. Like a baby, I swear. But she still goes to a shrink or I'll break every bone in her body. Speaking of opening night, this is one show I'm going to steal. You should see my mask. I look like the Phantom of the Opera. Half the audience is going to be moving away from me. Oh, look who just came in the room fresh from her bath with a piece of Sara Lee in her hand. Hold on, I gotta go smack her.

Dear Bess,

Your sister is easily the meanest woman in the world. She took my cheese cake. She's out of her mind drunk. I think I'll bite her.

Sal

Hello again. Tonight we're staying home and watching TV, although certain ex-movie queens think they're going out to kick up their heels. I'll kill her. Wait, I take it back. That's not funny. Love to your gang,

Belle

Sally Ross

Dear Jake,

   I still can't believe it's over, and that he's dead instead of me. Oh, Jake, I will get another chance, won't I? I'm so tired, my darling. So bitterly tired. Belle's with me now. I love you both so much. I must sleep now. I'll call you in the morning.

                                        Sal

Sally Ross

Thursday the 29th.

Dear Jake,

Well, the opening is finally here. An hour and a half away. My God, do you realize this is the first letter I've written you in two weeks! I wasn't kidding when I said I was swearing off writing letters. But tonight the circuits are busy and I think I already owe the telephone company my first month's percentage, which, incidentally, looks like it might be a bundle. I can't believe how well previews have gone! And that ending, Jake! They actually love it! As Belle would say, go know. Belle looks so cute in her gown and mask. Like the Lone Ranger in drag. Oh darling, I love you so much, and it's so wonderful to be normal again. I'm still ashamed of how I behaved, but I'm so gloriously happy! Belle is screaming that we've got to go. I'll finish this letter after the opening night party and that's a promise—Even if I can't see straight. Hold on, be back in a few hours! Have I mentioned I love you?

Dear Sally,

You will never read this letter, my darling. I am writing it for the world so that they will know that a love such as ours existed.

No, my darling, I am far from dead.

That charred body was not mine. It was the body of a sacrificial "lamb." I regretted having to end his life, but what else could I do? How else could I assure those around you that there was no further need for them? How else could I insure your return to the show? For both were necessary.

Lest the world deplore me for ending yet another life, it was at best a life this world should have been ashamed of. I chose carefully, not wanting to take the life of any who might prove to be a good decent person. And so I went to a "gay bar" and permitted myself to be leered at by the degenerates of that milieu. I carefully selected one of those lost souls and made his acquaintance. Then it was a simple matter to suggest he accompany me to a nearby rooftop, since I feigned a "lover" at home. I allowed as I would let him have his ungodly way with me if he came, and he did. There, on that previously selected rooftop, I permitted the unspeakable. On his knees in front of me, I looked down at him, much the way the prophets in the Bible looked down at their sacrificial lambs and I knew that my "pilgrimage" was as theirs had been. Theirs, for the love of God; mine, for the love of you.

The knife slid through his throat easily and he uttered no sound. The can of gasoline, previously hidden away, was near. I taped my letter to the roof door, "anointed" him and struck the match that would cause a fire of love that might prove to the world that nothing, not even death itself, is of any consequence when compared to the holiest of all things, love. For I do love you, Sally. No one can doubt that now.

I shall not mail this letter. It will be found in my jacket pocket after you and I share that most intimate of love acts, death. I shall be sitting in the first row at your opening tonight. The gun I carry will unite us for all eternity. You will die as you have lived, in the glory and glow of starlight, and I will die in the reflection of that glow. It is mere hours away now, Sally. Mere hours before no one and nothing can part us ever again. It is the same love that befell Romeo and Juliet. Like them, we shall live on in the hearts and minds of men for all time.

Sally, my own, my treasure, my beloved.

Douglas

THE END

Epilogue

The following letters arrived at Sally Ross's apartment the day after her death.

ARNO FLORIST
Sag Harbor

June 27, 1976

Dear Miss Ross:

I have been trying to contact Mr. Douglas Breen of 780
West 71st Street, New York City, without success in regard to the remainder of his bill. Mr. Breen sent me a
check for thirty-five dollars on account for flowers delivered
to the Water's Edge Inn on Saturday, May 26th. The manager of the inn told me you were to be Mr. Breen's companion for the weekend. The flowers were delivered but
there is still the matter of $25.35 due. I would appreciate
payment as soon as possible.

Sincerely yours,
Morton Fry

CONTINENTAL STUDIOS

June 29, 1976

Sal:

By the time you get this letter, I'll be somewhere over the Grand Canyon, facing east. Look for me after the show Friday night. Baby, now that you've proven whatever it was you had to prove, you can't stop me from coming. Besides, it's for *my* sake now. Heidi and I have decided to call it quits. She's a nice girl, but I don't think I can settle for a nice girl, after all. Not when I'm still used to a great one. I've got so much to say to you, Sal. I couldn't even start on the phone or I would've broken down and cried, which is why this letter. Look for me, darling. Friday night.

Jake

H

About the Author

BOB RANDALL lives in New York City
and has two children.
His plays include
6 RMS RIV VU, The Magic Show and *Odd Infinitum.*
The Fan is his first novel.